The Mystery
of the Dark
Lighthouse

Laura E. Williams

SCHOLASTIC INC.
New York Toronto London Auckland Sydney
Mexico City New Delhi Hong Kong Buenos Aires

This book is for Marilyn Cozad,

a fellow mystery buff

ISBN 0-439-21726-1

12 11 10 9 8 7 6 5 4 3 2 1   4 5 6 7 8 9/0

Printed in the U.S.A.   40

A Roundtable Press Book

For Roundtable Press, Inc.:
Directors: Julie Merberg, Marsha Melnick, Susan E. Meyer
Project Editor: Meredith Wolf Schizer
Computer Production: Carrie Glidden
Designer: Elissa Stein
Illustrator: Laura Maestro

Contents

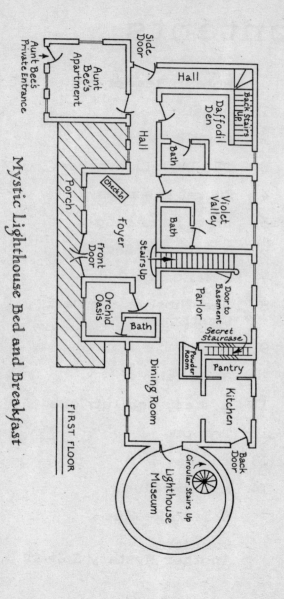

Mystic Lighthouse Bed and Breakfast

FIRST FLOOR

Side Door

Hall

Back Stairs Up

Daffodil Den

Bath

Aunt Bee's Apartment

Aunt Bee's Private Entrance

Hall

Check In

Porch

Violet Valley

Bath

Foyer

Stairs Up

Front Door

Door to Basement

Parlor

Orchid Oasis

Bath

Secret Staircase

Powder Room

Pantry

Dining Room

Kitchen

Back Door

Lighthouse Museum

Circular Stairs Up

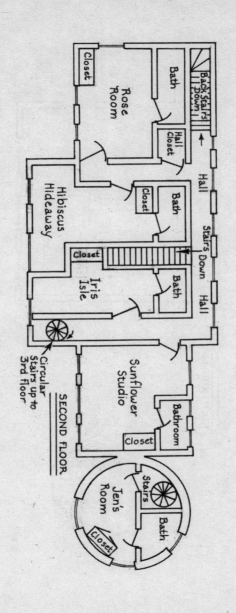

Closet

Bath

Rose Room

Back Stairs Down

Hall Closet

Hall

Closet

Bath

Hibiscus Hideaway

Stairs Down

Closet

Iris Isle

Bath

Hall

Circular Stairs Up to 3rd Floor

Sunflower Studio

SECOND FLOOR

Closet

Bathroom

Stairs

Jen's Room

Closet

Bath

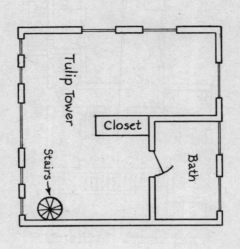

Tulip Tower

Closet

Bath

Stairs →

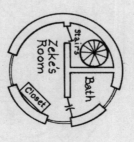

Zeke's Room

Stairs

Bath

Closet

Note to Reader

Welcome to *The Mystery of the Dark Lighthouse*, where YOU solve the mystery. As you read, look for clues pointing to the guilty person. There is a blank suspect sheet in the back of this book. You can copy it to keep track of the clues you find throughout the story. These are the same suspect sheets that Jen and Zeke will use later in the story when they try to solve the mystery. Can you solve *The Mystery of the Dark Lighthouse* before they can?

Good luck!

Ghost!

Completely out of breath, Jen flung open the front door of the Mystic Lighthouse Bed and Breakfast and raced inside. Her twin brother, Zeke, followed closely behind her. Aunt Bee handed each of them a towel. The twins had lived with their aunt in the B&B since their parents' death when they were only two years old. Uncle Cliff, Aunt Bee's husband, had died a couple of years ago, so Aunt Bee was all the family they had left.

"I hate this rain," Jen complained. Even with a raincoat on, she'd gotten soaked.

Zeke hung his dripping green slicker on the coat-rack, next to Jen's. He rubbed his hair with the warm, dry towel. "The Mystic bicentennial cookout will be canceled tomorrow."

"I'm afraid you're right," Aunt Bee agreed. "This is just the edge of the storm—it's supposed to pour all weekend. We may even get some hail."

With a towel draped across her damp shoulders, Jen stared outside into the stormy darkness. The trees twisted in the wind, and lightning flashed over the churning ocean. "I hope we don't lose power again."

"We always lose electricity being this far out," Zeke said glumly. "Not only will the storm keep me from sailing, I won't be able to play computer games, either."

Aunt Bee grinned. "But think of all the chores you'll get done!"

The twins worked hard to help their aunt keep the B&B running smoothly. Cleaning rooms was easy, and the guests were usually interesting to meet and talk to. Jen and Zeke also helped at mealtimes, especially if Aunt Bee was serving more than the usual breakfast that she offered the guests every day. Under special circumstances, Aunt Bee also prepared lunch and dinner for them.

Once they were somewhat dried off, the twins followed their aunt across the foyer to the check-in counter. There she had already laid out several flashlights, extra batteries, three oil lamps, and a number of candles. Flashlights were fine, Aunt Bee always said, but lamps and candles created a cozy old-time feel.

"Get into dry clothes, then come back and help me get these ready," Aunt Bee instructed, trimming one of the lamp wicks.

Zeke glanced at the registration book. "Have some people already checked in?" he asked.

"Lenore and Karen Mills are in the Sunflower Studio," Aunt Bee replied. "Driving from the airport in this weather wore them out and they're resting."

"Dead Man's Curve is bad enough on a sunny day," Zeke said, picturing the hairpin turns on the road to the B&B, with the cliff dropping off abruptly to the rocks and foaming ocean far below. Somehow the short guardrail along the edge didn't seem like enough protection. "It must be really bad driving around it on a day like this!"

"That's for sure," Jen agreed, heading out of the foyer toward her room. Zeke followed her through the large dining room to the circular lighthouse museum that occupied the bottom floor of the remodeled lighthouse tower. The eleven-year-old twins had helped design the museum, filling it with old photographs of the lighthouse, the nearby town of Mystic, Maine, and the Markham family, who had run the lighthouse for generations. Other memorabilia, such as old fishing tackle and some vintage foul-weather gear, were also on display.

Even though history wasn't one of Zeke's favorite subjects, digging into the history of the lighthouse had been fun. Besides, Aunt Bee knew everything there was to know about Mystic and its famous lighthouse. She had been the head librarian in town for many years. She claimed that she'd forgotten more facts than she remembered, but in Zeke's opinion she knew more than an encyclopedia.

At the back of the museum Uncle Cliff had installed a circular staircase. It wound past Jen's bedroom on the second floor and Zeke's on the third floor, all the way to the top platform of the lighthouse.

Jen went to her room, while Zeke climbed the extra flight to his. Jen had decorated her room with posters of athletes and a few of cats. In her usual style, none of the posters was hanging straight. In fact, they looked as if she had thrown them at the walls, sending them every which way. Zeke's posters of sailboats and *Star Wars* movies marched across his walls in a perfect line.

Zeke draped his wet clothes over the back of his desk chair to dry. He pulled on a green sweatshirt and gray sweatpants, and finally felt warm and dry. As he rubbed more water out of his dark, wavy hair, he peered out his window that overlooked the Atlantic Ocean. The second window in his room faced the bay.

The howling wind whipped the water below into white froth. Zeke shivered even though he wasn't cold. Sometimes the force of the stormy ocean gave him chills. *I wouldn't want to be out there in a boat*, he thought. Though he loved sailing and swimming, he knew how dangerous the ocean could be, especially in this weather.

His hair felt fairly dry, and after running his fingers through it, he rushed back down to Jen's room. When she opened her door, he saw that she had left her wet clothes in a soggy pile in the middle of the floor. Typical Jen. But he knew better than to say anything about it.

As they hurried through the dining room, the lights flickered. The twins looked at each other, waiting for the inevitable to happen, but the lights stayed on.

Zeke groaned. "I just know it. We're going to lose power."

They continued through the parlor and joined Aunt Bee in the foyer. She took one look at them and smiled. "You two look like mice on a sinking ship. Why so glum?" Then she held up her hand for silence as Jen and Zeke started in about the rain and being cooped up and having no electricity. "Forget I asked," she said with a laugh. "It's not the end of the world. Maybe we won't lose power after all—"

As though on cue, thunder crackled close by. The lights flickered, then went out. The thick gray clouds outside blocked all the sunlight. With the lights off, it was so dark it felt like midnight to the twins, even though it was only three o'clock in the afternoon.

Jen heard the scrape of a match, and Aunt Bee's face reappeared, glowing in the soft light of one of the oil lamps. She adjusted the wick and grinned at them.

"The adventure begins," she said, lighting two more lamps. "Could you two prepare the other three rooms while I deliver these lights to our resting guests?"

Zeke snapped on a flashlight as Aunt Bee left the foyer, guided by her flickering lamp. The twins headed toward the front stairs. Linens and towels were kept in the bottom drawer of the dresser in each room. The quilts, sheets, and towels were coordinated to match each room's unique floral theme. It made preparing the rooms a lot easier.

They had just mounted the first step when Zeke stopped. "Did you hear that?" he whispered hoarsely.

"Hear what? It's probably just the wind blowing something around outside."

Zeke gripped her arm. "Shhhhh!"

"I don't hear anything." But as soon as the words were out of her mouth, Jen heard a strange thump. There was no way the wind could make a noise like that *inside* the B&B.

The twins stared at each other with wide eyes,

and Jen's heart started to hammer. "What was that?"

"It came from the parlor," answered Zeke.

"It's probably just Woofer," Jen said.

Zeke shook his head and aimed his flashlight toward the check-in counter. Woofer, their Old English sheepdog, lay beside it with his head resting on his paws. Slinky, their huge Maine coon cat, was curled up on top of the dog. It was their favorite way to nap.

Another dull thump came from the parlor.

Jen grabbed the light out of Zeke's hand and started to tiptoe in that direction. Zeke had no choice but to follow his sister since she had control of the flashlight.

They rounded the corner. The parlor piano and furniture looked like shadowy lumps—or crouching monsters. Then, in a nearly blinding flash of lightning, followed immediately by the crack of thunder, the twins saw a girl standing by the wall, her pale face staring back at them. The room went dark again. By the time Jen swerved the flashlight to the spot where the girl had stood along the wall, the girl was gone!

Double Take

"Did you see that?" Jen gasped. Then she gave a little shriek as something wound around her ankles. It took her a second to realize it wasn't a ghostly hand, but Slinky.

"See what?" asked Zeke.

"That girl! She—she looked like a ghost."

"It must have been a trick of the light," Zeke said, not sounding too sure of himself.

"So you *did* see her?"

Reluctantly, Zeke nodded until he realized it was too dark for his sister to see him. "I saw her, but only for a second."

"She disappeared into thin air. Did you see her face?" Jen asked, her voice still low.

"Yup," Zeke said, swallowing hard. "She didn't look too happy."

"An angry ghost."

Zeke wished his sister hadn't said that. After all, they had heard strange noises in the lighthouse tower before—soft laughter, the creak of floorboards, odd whistling. There was even an old legend in town about a ghost who blew out the flame in the lighthouse so that ships would wreck on the rocks below. Even though that story was good for a few chills, they'd never actually seen or heard anything menacing. Until now.

"Maybe we just imagined it," Zeke said.

"No way," Jen protested, a shiver trickling up her spine. "I saw her. She looked right at me."

Zeke tugged his sister's arm. "Come on, we have to get the rooms ready."

Reluctantly, Jen let her brother lead her upstairs. Had she really seen a ghost? She couldn't think about anything else as they checked the Rose Room, making sure the bed was neatly made and the bathroom was in order, with pink towels hanging evenly on the rack. Aunt Bee liked to call the B&B her "flower-filled hive" because of all the floral patterns everywhere—on pillows, wallpaper, lampshades, and curtains. When Zeke tried to explain to her that a hive was full of honey, not flowers, Aunt Bee had simply said that at sixty-two years old she could fill her hive with flowers if she wanted to. After all, she'd added, honey was made from flowers, and wasn't she a "Bee"?

By the time they got to the room they called the Hibiscus Hideaway, the storm had gotten worse. It was slamming loose branches against the windows and pushing cold air through every crack, creating eerie moans and whistles. When they finished preparing the Hibiscus Hideaway, they moved downstairs to the Violet Valley, which was just off the foyer. This was Jen's favorite guest room because it was decorated in purple: purple flowered wallpaper, purple striped curtains, a purple painted dresser—even the towels in the bathroom were purple. Purple was Jen's favorite color.

When they came out of the room, Aunt Bee was busy at the check-in counter. Before her stood a middle-aged couple in raincoats that dripped water on the floor around them. The tall man looked like a giant next to the short, round woman with him. The woman sneezed three times in a row, then rummaged through her large red canvas handbag and retrieved a crumpled tissue.

Aunt Bee asked, "Have you had that cold long, Mrs. Snyder?"

"Excuse me?" Mrs. Snyder said, cupping a hand to her ear.

"How long have you been sick?" Aunt Bee asked, raising her voice above the storm.

"Oh, not long. A day or two," Mrs. Snyder nearly shouted back. "It's just the sniffles."

As the twins approached, Aunt Bee introduced them to the new guests.

"Professor Snyder is writing a book about Maine," Aunt Bee explained.

Professor Snyder looked down at them through gold-rimmed glasses and smiled under his salt-and-pepper mustache. "It's been very interesting so far. I'm especially looking forward to the Mystic bicentennial celebration."

"But it'll get canceled because of the storm," Jen blurted out.

The professor's face fell. "I've come all this way."

Aunt Bee nodded. "I'm afraid Jen is right. The storm has also caused two couples to cancel their reservations with us."

The professor looked even more upset. "Oh, no."

"You're welcome to cancel your reservation," Aunt Bee offered. "I'd certainly understand."

"No, no, we've come this far," Professor Snyder said reluctantly.

"Then just sign in here," Aunt Bee said as she pointed to the registration book, "and then the twins will help you to your room."

Jen reached for Mrs. Snyder's overnight bag, which was also made of red canvas, and hefted it in her right hand.

"These people have already checked in?" the professor asked, his pen poised above the registration book.

"That's right, Lenore Mills and her daughter," Aunt Bee confirmed, peering at the open book. "They're upstairs, but you'll be meeting them at dinner."

Professor Snyder beamed. "How delightful."

As Zeke started to reach for his suitcase, the professor snatched it. "This is too heavy for you, young man. It's full of my research books. Just point the way and I'll take care of it."

Zeke felt his face burn. He knew he could carry the bag. But he was sure the professor wouldn't appreciate his wrestling the suitcase away from him, so Zeke simply led the couple to the Violet Valley.

Jen set Mrs. Snyder's suitcase on the bench at the foot of the bed as both Snyders admired the room decor. Aunt Bee, Uncle Cliff, and the twins had put a lot of thought into planning everything about the B&B, from the artwork on the walls to the size of the dining room table.

Professor Snyder carefully placed his oversized suitcase against the wall and tested the bed for firmness. He nodded with approval. "This will do just fine," he said. He handed each of the twins a crisp dollar bill and closed the door on their backs.

The twins joined their aunt at the check-in counter just as the front door opened and another guest stepped in. She tried to shut the door behind her but the wind pushed back and for a second it looked as if the wind might win.

With a loud "Oof," the woman shoved the door closed. "Nice weather," she commented with a wry grin as she approached. "And no electricity," she added, noting the oil lamp on the counter and the flashlight in Zeke's hand.

"Just pretend you've stepped back in time," Aunt Bee suggested, "and you'll have a marvelous time."

The woman shivered. "How delightful. I always wondered what it would be like to live in the 1800s."

She patted her straight black hair as if to make sure the wind hadn't blown it away. It was surprisingly neat and hung down to her shoulders. Her narrow face had at first looked serious, but as soon as she smiled, her eyes lit up like twinkling stars.

Aunt Bee stared openly at the newest guest until even Jen noticed her staring and coughed. Aunt Bee laughed and focused on the registration process. "I'm sorry, Mrs. Barr," she said. "But you look so familiar to me."

"I just have one of those faces that looks familiar, that's all. And please, call me Esther."

"I'm sure that's it," Aunt Bee said lightly. "Now, if you'll just sign in, Zeke will show you to the Rose Room on the second floor."

Just as Zeke was about to head up the stairs with Esther Barr, the front door blew open and a tall man rushed in, slamming the door shut behind him. Jen stared at him. Even though she didn't watch much TV, she recognized him immediately. It was Jaspar Westcombe, the famous television reporter who did special assignments for the national news. Jen remembered that his last special had been about an Egyptian tomb filled with gold statues. She would know his suntanned, chiseled face anywhere. Even in the storm, his blond hair was smooth and slicked back—just like on TV. She was so amazed that she didn't notice the way he did a double take when he spied Esther standing at the foot of the stairs. But Zeke did. He also saw that Esther quickly turned away from the reporter with a look of panic on her face and rushed up the stairs.

The Dark Lighthouse

Jen tried not to stare as Jaspar Westcombe introduced himself to Aunt Bee.

"Are you on assignment?" Jen asked, inching closer.

Jaspar laughed. "Oh, no. I'm just here for a relaxing weekend. I've been working too hard and I need some R&R—rest and relaxation."

"That's what we're here for," Aunt Bee sang out. "R&R at the B&B."

Jen took one of the reporter's bags and led him upstairs to his room.

"You're in the Hibiscus Hideaway," she said as she aimed her flashlight at the floor so he wouldn't trip. When she opened the door to his room, he whistled in appreciation. The best part of this room was a live hibiscus bush with three orange blooms on it in an enormous pale green ceramic pot. The blossoms were closing up a bit, but they were still pretty and fragrant.

"This is great," he said. "Thanks for your help." He handed Jen a two-dollar tip.

Jen met Zeke at the top of the stairs and they headed down together. She told him about their famous guest.

Then Zeke told her about Esther Barr's reaction to seeing Jaspar Westcombe enter the foyer. "As soon as she saw him, she became nervous and edgy."

"She even acted weird when Aunt Bee said she looked familiar," Jen said. She was about to say more, but the grandfather clock in the dining room bonged six times, cutting her off. Aunt Bee called to them from the kitchen. She needed their help in preparing a light supper of clam chowder and steaming-hot biscuits for the guests. Even though there was no electricity for lights or to pump up the water from the well, they could still cook because Aunt Bee had a gas oven and a gas-powered refrigerator. Because the electricity went out so easily during a storm, she had switched to gas so she could still feed her guests.

When the meal was ready, Zeke knocked on all the doors and told the guests that the food would be left on the sideboard in the dining room for a couple of hours, being kept warm with a Sterno food heater. He invited them to help themselves when they got hungry. When he returned to the dining room, he found Jen and Aunt Bee already eating, so he joined them. He dug into his chowder. No doubt about it, Aunt Bee was the best cook in Mystic.

⌒⌄

After they ate, the twins retreated to Jen's room to finish a game of Monopoly they'd been playing earlier.

"I am the champion!" Zeke crowed when he finally bankrupted Jen.

Jen grinned. "Just wait till next time, Mr. Champion. I have a whole new strategy planned."

Zeke laughed. "You always say that and you always lose. Come on, Aunt Bee probably wants us to wash the dishes."

When they got downstairs, they were surprised to see the dining room and kitchen already spotless.

"There you are," Aunt Bee said, swishing her long gray braid out of the way as she ran a towel over the counter one last time. "Hiding on me?"

"No!" Jen exclaimed. "We were in my room, playing—"

"I was only teasing," Aunt Bee said with a laugh. "The guests finished early, so I cleaned up without you. But I did save the best job. Normally I'd say you should wait till it stops raining, but I don't think that's going to happen for awhile. If you take out the garbage now, you won't have to worry about it again till Monday. By then, the storm should have blown itself out."

The twins each lugged one heavy bag out the back door of the kitchen. In the beating rain, they hurried to the side of the B&B where they kept the trash bins. Jen clenched her teeth, feeling the cold water trickle under her hood.

After they'd dumped their load, they raced around to the front of the building. Jen suddenly stopped and looked up at the B&B, trying to protect her eyes from the slashing rain. The glimmer of oil lamps shone from several windows, but the lighthouse tower was dark. Aunt Bee usually kept the electric lamp at the top of the lighthouse lit, even though it wasn't an official lighthouse anymore. She did it for the historical feel it gave the B&B, she said. And even though there were electronic sounding systems to warn ships and boats away from the dangerous rocks and cliffs, local fishermen said they loved to see the lighthouse when they were out late. It gave them a sense of comfort and welcome as they headed home in their boats.

Now with the power out, the lighthouse looked eerie. Jen shivered, imagining what it must have been like in the old days, trying to find the safe harbor in a storm without a beacon from the lighthouse. One wrong turn and the ship would crash against the rocks.

When they got inside, Jen told Zeke how creepy she thought the dark lighthouse would have been in the old days.

"But the light wasn't run by electricity back then," Zeke reminded her. "It was the lighthouse keeper's job to make sure the oil lamp didn't burn out."

"What if the lighthouse keeper was sick or something?"

Zeke shrugged. "Maybe he had an assistant." He looked around. The B&B was quiet. "I guess Aunt Bee went to bed," he commented.

"Everyone else must be asleep, too," Jen whispered as they peeled off their coats and hung them up on the pegs near the front door.

Zeke yawned as he flicked on the small flashlight he'd kept in his pocket. "I guess I'll go to bed, too. I can't work on the computer, I can't watch TV, and I can't—"

"Oh, stop complaining," Jen interrupted. "I have a great idea."

Zeke looked at his twin doubtfully. Jen wasn't known for her great ideas. "What is it?"

"Let's go look for the ghost! Come on," Jen urged,

her blue eyes flashing. "It'll be fun."

"Looking for a ghost doesn't sound like fun to me. It sounds crazy."

"Then I'm going alone," Jen said, starting off through the dimly lit foyer.

"Wait." The beam from the flashlight bobbed on the floor ahead of Zeke as he caught up. "I'll go with you."

Silently, they searched the foyer, then the parlor and the dining room.

"Forget it," Zeke said. "There's no ghost. We must have imagined it before." As the words left his mouth, they heard a crash in the kitchen.

Jen raced forward with Zeke following two feet behind her. He aimed the flashlight around the room. Nothing.

Jen tugged on his sleeve and pointed to the open pantry. "In there!" she whispered excitedly.

Tiptoeing, hearts slamming against their ribs, they nervously made their way to the opening in the pantry. Taking a deep breath, Zeke shined his light in.

The beam fell on a pale, shimmering figure.

Secret Passages

Zeke dropped the flashlight and it blinked and went out. The pantry was pitch-black. Jen dove for the last place she had seen the flashlight. Other hands were reaching around at the same time. Their fingers got tangled. Finally Zeke got hold of the flashlight and switched it on.

The pale girl hadn't disappeared. She stood there, glaring at them. And in the glow of the flashlight, they could see that she had long, reddish-brown hair. "Don't shine that light in my eyes," she said crossly.

Zeke lowered the beam. "Who are you?"

"Karen Mills. I'm staying here with my mom. Who are you?"

"Jen and Zeke. We live here," Jen answered. "What are you doing?"

The girl's gaze flitted around the dark pantry. "I—

uh—was looking for something to eat."

Jen and Zeke glanced at each other.

"I'm not hungry anymore," Karen said, edging by them to get out of the pantry. "I'll see you later." With that she sprinted out of the kitchen and the twins heard her footsteps fade quickly.

"What was she doing here?" Jen wondered aloud. "I'm sure she wasn't looking for food."

Zeke silently agreed with his sister. He looked at the cans of stewed tomatoes and jars of homegrown string beans. "Something about her is so familiar," Zeke added as he examined the wall of pantry shelves where Karen had been standing. What had she been looking for?

Finally he gave up the search. Nothing looked out of the ordinary or out of place. They headed toward their bedrooms.

Zeke shrugged his shoulders. "There's something strange about Karen."

Jen yawned. "Like what?"

As they walked through the lighthouse museum, Jen headed straight for the circular stairs. But Zeke stood in the museum, sweeping the beam of light from his flashlight across the wall of old photographs. His light finally settled on one yellowed photograph in its original silver frame.

"Look," he called to Jen.

She came beside him and looked at the photograph. She remembered finding the photo in an old trunk in the attic. It was a picture of a young girl standing in front of a Christmas tree, holding a teddy bear in her arms. Jen's blood froze in her veins. "That's—that's her! That's Karen Mills!"

Zeke peered at the inscription etched in the silver frame. "No, it's Catherine Markham, the daughter of the original lighthouse keeper. That must have been about 1900."

"But they could be identical twins!"

Zeke agreed. "I knew she looked familiar. But this is really spooky."

Jen shivered. "Karen's not a ghost, though. Right?"

"When she brushed past us as she left the pantry, she didn't feel like a ghost," Zeke said. "She felt warm and solid like a human being."

"We have to find out what's going on," Jen said, forgetting how tired she'd felt only minutes before.

Zeke checked his watch. "It's too late now."

"It's only ten o'clock!" Jen protested, glancing over his shoulder at the glowing dial.

"Everyone's already in bed. If we wake up a guest Aunt Bee won't be too thrilled. We'll just have to start first thing tomorrow."

Jen woke up Saturday morning to the sounds of not-so-distant thunder, rain pelting against her windows, and storm-driven waves crashing into the cliff below. She snuggled deeper under her quilt. This was a perfect day to stay cuddled up with a good book.

She suddenly sprang out of bed. How could she lie there when there was a ghostly look-alike eating breakfast downstairs? She threw on a wrinkled T-shirt and a pair of sweatpants. Then she ran her fingers through her hair, pushed her feet into her favorite pair of old sneakers, and rushed down to the dining room.

Zeke was already there, helping Aunt Bee set up the coffee and juice table and arranging the fresh rolls and muffins on the dining room table. A warm, cheery fire roared in the fireplace. Woofer was sleeping on the small rug in front of the hearth, but Slinky was nowhere to be seen. Nor had the cat slept with Jen the previous night, which was unusual. Unease rippled through her, but she shrugged it off. Slinky was smarter than most humans and knew how to stay out of trouble. Usually.

Jen put out the homemade jams and jellies and a dish of butter. The muffins smelled awesome; her favorite kind was banana macadamia nut. As soon as everything was set up, she grabbed one, along with a glass of orange juice, and settled at the dining room table as the guests trickled in.

Aunt Bee greeted each person by name, explaining the variety of freshly baked muffins and rolls. The twins sat side by side, inspecting the guests as they made their breakfast choices. At one point Jen nudged Zeke in the ribs. "Look at that," she whispered.

Zeke turned to see Jaspar Westcombe heading straight for Esther Barr, who was choosing a muffin. When Jaspar tapped her to get her attention, she looked up, startled. *Was that a flash of fear in her eyes?* Jen wondered.

Aunt Bee clapped her hands for attention. "I'm so sorry about the electricity still being out. It's back on in town, but if the storm continues, it may go out again. Unfortunately, we're a ways out of town and always the last ones to get power restored. I'm so sorry."

"It's delightful," Esther said, waving her hand. "It makes me feel like I'm living long ago."

Zeke noticed that as she talked, Esther edged away from Jaspar and sat down at the table between Jen and a thin, pale woman whose hair was the same reddish-brown color as Karen Mills's hair. Karen sat on the other side of the thin woman—she was obviously Karen's mother. Esther nervously touched a hand to her bangs, brushing a lock away from her face. Now there was no way for Jaspar to get to her without being rude or overly obvious. But why was the investigative reporter chasing her?

"How on earth did you bake these delicious goodies?" Mrs. Snyder asked. She and her husband had come in, filled their plates, and settled on the other side of Karen Mills.

Aunt Bee smiled at them in the candlelight. "I had a gas oven and refrigerator installed after the last big storm. We won't run out of food here. And I'm planning on serving all three meals for anyone interested, since getting into town will be a rather wet adventure. Even if you drive, you'll have to park and walk to the shops. You're sure to get soaked. I do have extra umbrellas for any brave souls, however. . . ."

Aunt Bee continued with her morning speech while Jen zoned out. She'd heard it all before. When all the guests had helped themselves, Aunt Bee made a small plate for herself and joined the others around the large dining room table. Aunt Bee liked her guests to mingle, so she served all the meals family-style at one large table. She looked around as she always did, making sure everyone had everything they needed. Staring at Karen Mills, she said, "Did you know you look remarkably like a girl in one of the photos in the lighthouse museum?"

Karen's mother laughed lightly. "I noticed that when I was wandering around yesterday. As a matter of fact, Catherine Markham is my great-great-aunt. Karen has her old diary."

"Really?" asked Professor Snyder. "How interesting. I would love to see it. It would be a marvelous research source for my book."

"What, dear?" Mrs. Snyder said. "Did you say something?"

Professor Snyder raised his voice. "Nothing, dear."

"Why don't you tell everyone about it?" Mrs. Mills suggested to her scowling daughter.

"It's not that interesting," Karen said curtly, crossing her arms.

Mrs. Mills chuckled. "She's being modest. Karen has read it more than ten times." She lowered her voice. "The diary even talks about secret passageways and hidden rooms in this old place."

Jen and Zeke looked at each other. *Secret passages!*

"I've heard those rumors," Aunt Bee said. "But I've been living here for years and I haven't found anything of the sort, I'm sorry to say. Every square foot is pretty well accounted for."

"That's what I said," Mrs. Mills remarked, looking at her daughter. "But she's been dying to visit the lighthouse ever since she first read the old diary. I thought this bicentennial celebration would be a good time to come."

"How sad that most of the events will be canceled because of the weather and the power failure," Aunt Bee said. "But I'd be happy to take anyone on a tour of our historic town this weekend, and certainly of the B&B as well."

"That would be fun. Maybe we'll find old Aunt Catherine's treasure," Mrs. Mills said, grinning at her daughter.

At these words, Karen gave her mother a dark glare.

"Treasure?" Jen piped in. "What treasure?"

"Never mind," Karen said before her mother could open her mouth. "There is no treasure."

Jen caught Zeke's eye and knew what he was thinking. *Karen is lying!* Now they knew why she was poking around in the pantry.

5

Up to Something

Esther Barr clapped her hands. "A treasure! How perfect."

"There is no treasure," Karen insisted.

"Oh, I'm sure there must be," Esther said. Her straight black hair swung from side to side. "It's just what I was hoping for."

"Why?" Zeke asked.

Esther looked startled. "Oh, no reason. Just my silly imagination getting away from me."

"A lighthouse treasure, now that's interesting," Jaspar said. Jen noticed a gleam in his eyes. A moment later, he excused himself. As he walked out of the dining room, Jen saw him pull a cell phone out of his jacket pocket.

Professor Snyder was chuckling softly. "A treasure," he finally said. "What a wonderful fantasy.

Unfortunately, it is completely impossible."

"Why is it impossible?" Karen demanded.

Jen noticed that Karen sounded disappointed even though she'd just insisted that there wasn't a treasure.

"As you all know, I'm writing a book on Maine, and I have done a great deal of research on the small coastal towns like Mystic. Believe me, there is no mention of a treasure left by some pirate. Mystic wasn't even a very important port, which is why this lighthouse stopped being used quite early."

"That's correct," Aunt Bee agreed, beginning to clear away the dishes. Jen and Zeke hopped up to help. "My husband and I had to put electricity in the lighthouse ourselves."

"What did they use before that?" Mrs. Mills asked.

Professor Snyder cleared his throat and began speaking as though he were giving a lecture to a room full of students. "Before electricity, lighthouses used whale oil lamps, which the lighthouse keeper had to keep filled. Some lights were stationary and didn't revolve. Others were wound up with a clockwork mechanism so that the lights turned in circles."

"What if the keeper forgot to fill the oil lamps?" Jen asked.

The professor turned to her, his gray eyebrows pressing low over his eyes. "Then ships crashed against the shore and lives were lost."

Jen shuddered and the dishes in her arms wobbled. Quickly she brought them into the kitchen. *Ships sank and lives were lost.*

Zeke came up behind her with an empty pitcher.

Jen whirled around. "Jeez, don't sneak up on me like that."

"Why are you so jumpy?"

"I was just thinking about all those poor sailors looking for the light after long, long days at sea, then not seeing the dangerous rocks and cliffs till they had crashed into them."

"It's like the town legend about the ghost who blew out the lamps, leaving the lighthouse dark," Zeke mused.

"And now the lighthouse is dark again," Jen said, feeling an odd fear tightening her throat. "Just like long ago. . . ." She let her voice trail off.

For a second, Zeke stood spellbound. Then he shook himself. "You should be a writer," he said, chuckling. He headed out of the kitchen.

Jen filled a pot of water from the bucket by the back door. The water was from the outside well. She turned on the gas burner, using a match to ignite the flame, and then placed the pot on the stove. She stood by the stove, waiting for the water to warm up so that she could wash the dishes. Zeke took his time clearing away the rest of the breakfast dishes as the guests made plans for the day.

"Karen and I are going into town," Lenore Mills said, still sipping her coffee.

"But it's raining," Karen protested.

Mrs. Mills laughed. "I don't think you'll melt from a little rain."

"It's more than a little," Karen grumbled.

"Excuse me?" Mrs. Snyder said loudly, pointing to her ear. "I didn't quite catch that."

"Never mind," Professor Snyder said to his wife. He stood up and his wife followed suit. "I have some work to do in my room," he told the others.

"I'll just relax in the parlor," Mrs. Snyder said, digging a paperback book out of her huge red purse.

After they left, Esther rose gracefully. "I'm just going to mosey around the old place, if you don't mind. This is such a fascinating setting." With that, she strolled out of the dining room, looking around with interest at the furniture, the pictures on the walls, and the views from the windows.

Zeke carried his load into the kitchen, where the water had finally heated and Jen was now washing the dishes. She flung soap suds at him.

Aunt Bee appeared at that moment and put her

hands on her hips. "I saw that."

Jen tried to defend herself, but she knew her aunt wasn't really angry. In fact, Jen reasoned, the one good suds fight they'd had last summer, Aunt Bee had started!

"Zeke, get me the scissors from the front desk, please," Aunt Bee asked.

Zeke jogged through the dining room and into the foyer. He stopped in his tracks when he heard Esther Barr's voice. As he neared the desk, Esther's silky voice became louder and louder, and Zeke realized she must be just down the hall near the Daffodil Den. He strained his ears, trying to listen.

". . . do anything to get that treasure. Absolutely anything . . . hunt for it night and day, and do whatever is necessary to find it. . . ."

Zeke gulped. He grabbed the scissors and hurried back to the kitchen.

As soon as Aunt Bee left, he quickly told Jen what he'd overheard. Her eyes widened. "I knew there was something suspicious about her. Who was she talking to?"

"I don't know. I didn't hear another voice. Maybe she has a cell phone."

Jen wiped the last dish and placed it on the rack to dry. "Come on, let's see if she's still talking."

As they made their way into the dining room,

they heard Mrs. Mills set down her coffee cup at the far end of the room and say, "Let's go, honey."

"Uh, I don't feel so hot, Mom," Karen said.

Zeke and Jen backtracked a few steps into the museum and peeked around the door.

Karen was making a face that, even in the spotty lighting, Jen recognized immediately as a "faking being sick" face. She'd tried it a few times herself.

Mrs. Mills must have seen it before, too, because she narrowed her eyes at her daughter. "Are you sure?"

"The town is quite lovely," Aunt Bee added as she walked into the dining room.

Karen looked even sicker. "I'm sure it is. I'll just go lie down."

With a shrug of defeat, Mrs. Mills pulled on a lavender raincoat. Jen loved the color, and saw that it looked great with Mrs. Mills's pale complexion and pretty hair. Then the twins lost sight of her as she headed into the foyer with Aunt Bee.

Now the dining room was empty. Karen looked around nervously, not noticing Jen and Zeke watching her from behind the museum door. She picked up a flashlight. Instead of heading in the direction of her room, she tiptoed into the kitchen.

"She's up to something," Jen hissed. She stepped stealthily after Karen, Zeke close behind. They moved silently into the kitchen. Empty. Jen pointed to the pantry and put a finger over her lips. Zeke nodded. They were sure they would find Karen where they had found her last night. Taking care to move as quietly as possible, they slid into the pantry.

Jen gasped. Karen had disappeared!

A Valuable Secret

"I knew it!" Jen exclaimed, forgetting to keep her voice down. "She *is* a ghost!"

Zeke was examining the shelves as he had last night. He pressed and tugged and jiggled them. "You're nuts, you know that?" he said as he continued to work. "Karen is *not* a ghost. There has to be a logical explanation for this. Get me a flashlight."

For once, Jen didn't argue. She shone the light for him. Suddenly, he went still and cocked his head.

"Hear that?"

Jen strained her ears. Yes! It was a muffled meowing sound. "Hey, that's Slinky, and it sounds as if she's behind the wall!"

Zeke resumed his inspection of the shelves and the wall, pressing and poking everywhere. "Hey, shine the light over here. See the gap?"

"Maybe it's a hidden door," Jen said, tingling with excitement.

Zeke pushed the canned tomatoes out of the way and ran his fingers along the edge of the narrow slit. Nothing.

"Try again," Jen urged.

Concentrating, Zeke pressed harder, hoping he wouldn't get a splinter from the old wood. Suddenly, an entire three-foot-wide section of the wall swung backward, leaving a black hole.

Slinky streaked out, covered with dust.

Jen lunged for the cat, but Slinky disappeared around the corner faster than a lightning bolt.

"How long has she been back there?" Jen wondered out loud. "She didn't sleep with me, so she must have been stuck back there all night."

Zeke wasn't listening. "A secret tunnel!"

Jen whirled around and peered into the dark gap. Without pausing she lunged forward, eager to see what was inside.

Zeke pulled her back. "Be careful," he said. "You don't know what's back there."

"Obviously Karen went in here. Come on." She stepped lightly into the dark, narrow passage. Almost immediately they came upon a staircase leading down. Jen flashed her light down the stairs, but the steps seemed to go on forever. She wasn't so eager anymore.

Zeke gave her a nudge. "Well? Are you going or not?"

"I guess so." Taking a deep breath, as though it might be her last, Jen started down.

Zeke stayed close behind, counting the steps as they went. When the stairs didn't stop at fifteen, the way the stairs into the basement did, he realized they were going to a level *below* the basement.

"It's cold down here," Jen said, shivering.

Zeke touched the wall. "This passageway was carved out of stone."

"The steps are wood," Jen commented. "And they're pretty dusty and dirty. But these footprints look like they were made recently."

"They must be Karen's," Zeke said.

At last they reached the bottom of the stairs.

"I feel like a character in a fairy tale or a fantasy story," Jen whispered. Ahead of them were two openings. She shined the light to the left. "Those stairs go up." Aiming the flashlight forward she saw that the ground was level. "Let's go this way."

They crept along. Zeke tried not to think about the rough walls closing in on him, or the fact that they were at least twenty feet underground. The air was musty, but every once in a while he swore he felt a slight breeze that smelled of fresh air and salt water. The tunnel twisted and turned, completely disorienting him.

Soon they came to a three-way fork in the tunnel. To the right they saw another staircase leading down. The paths straight ahead and to the left looked like continuous tunnels.

"Which way did Karen go?" Jen asked.

As if to answer her question, they heard a soft sneeze. Jen motioned straight ahead with her flashlight and they hurried on. Just around a bend the light fell on Karen, who was trying to hold back another sneeze. When she saw them, she let the sneeze go.

"Gesundheit," Zeke said.

Karen frowned at them. "What are you two doing down here?"

"We followed you," Jen explained. "We want to know why you're snooping around. And how did you find these tunnels?"

"I'm not snooping, just exploring," Karen said defensively.

"Well, you disappeared last night in the parlor," Jen replied. "The way you just took off made it look like snooping to me."

"Never mind," Zeke interrupted. "The point is that you found these secret tunnels, and now we've found you. But don't worry," he added hastily when he saw the worried look on Karen's face. "We won't tell anyone. Right, Jen?"

"Of course not," Jen snapped. Then she relaxed and her face cracked a small grin. "This is way too interesting to share."

Karen eyed the twins doubtfully for a long moment. "Okay, I'll tell you the truth. But you have to swear not to tell anyone."

Jen and Zeke nodded.

"It's true that I have Catherine Markham's diary," Karen went on. "That's how I found out about these secret tunnels. As soon as we got here yesterday, I started looking around. That's it."

"That's it?" Jen repeated doubtfully.

"What about the treasure?" Zeke pressed. "Is there one?"

Karen still looked worried.

"You can tell us," Jen said. "We'll help you find it."

"So far all I've found are three entrances into the tunnels: from the parlor, the pantry, and an empty guest room."

"Cool!" Jen exclaimed. "We've lived here for years and never even knew. I can't believe Aunt Bee never found the secret entrances."

"But is there really a treasure?" Zeke asked.

Karen shrugged. "I haven't found anything. One

of the passages at the second fork goes to a room with old shelves along the walls, like a storage room. The other passage goes down even deeper." She grinned shyly. "But I was too chicken to check it out. And this one comes straight here, as you know. I haven't found any gold or anything yet, though."

"Gold?" Jen said with a gasp.

"I doubt it." Karen took a deep breath as though she were making a hard decision. "I should probably tell you something else. Catherine's diary ended abruptly. This is her last entry." She closed her eyes and recited as though she were reading the words behind her eyelids. *The mystery of the dark lighthouse is too awful to bear. If only I could confide in someone. But with so much wealth at stake, whom might I trust? Therefore, I must leave the truth for someone to find many years from now. Then all shall be discovered. I will hide the valuable secret as best I can, in case I need it someday. As always, X marks the spot to the left.*"

"The dark lighthouse again," Zeke said with a shudder. He quickly told Karen the town legends about a ghost blowing out the lamps and making the lighthouse dark and dangerous. "I wonder what Catherine knew about it."

"Her secret obviously has something to do with the hidden treasure," Jen said, her voice squeaky with

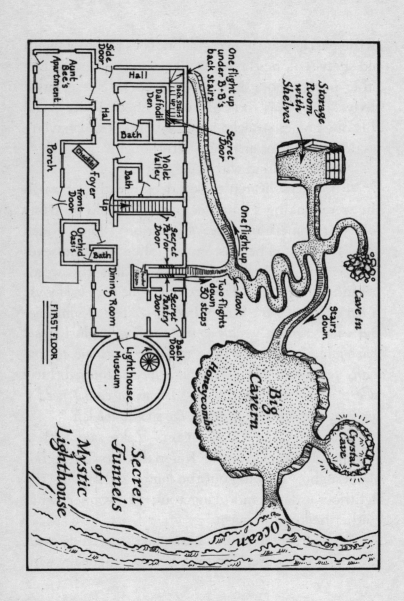

Secret Tunnels of Mystic Lighthouse

Cave in

Storage Room with Shelves

One flight up under B·B's back stairs

Back Stairs 1 up 2 up

Hall

Side Door

Aunt Bee's Apartment

Daffodil Den

Bath

Hall

Secret Door

Violet Valley

Bath

Porch

Checkin

foyer

Front Door

Up

Secret Parlor Door

Orchid Oasis

Bath

One flight up

Nook

Two flights down 30 steps

Secret Pantry Door

Dining Room

Back Door

Stairs down

Lighthouse Museum

FIRST FLOOR

Honeycombs

Big Cavern

Crystal Cave

Ocean

excitement. "We have to find the treasure to uncover her secret."

"And the only way to do that," Zeke added, "is to solve the clues that Catherine left in her diary."

"Well, we'd better hurry," Karen said sharply.

Jen looked at her. "Why?"

"I found a digging pick just beyond here."

"One of the picks they used to dig the tunnels?" Zeke asked.

Karen shook her head. "No. The pick wasn't there last night. There can only be one explanation for it."

"One of the other guests has found the tunnels and is looking for the treasure!" Jen and Zeke practically said in unison.

Karen nodded. "But who?"

X Marks the Spot

"Where's the pick?" Zeke asked.

Karen led them deeper into the tunnel, which ended suddenly.

"Looks like a cave-in," Jen said uneasily, eyeing the tumbled rocks and dirt blocking the passage. "I hope the rest of the tunnel doesn't collapse."

Karen agreed as she shone her light on the pick. Zeke crouched down to examine the dirty wooden handle and the sharp metal point.

"It looks old, but these shiny scratches show that it's been used recently against something hard, like these stone walls. The rocks scraped off the rust and dirt."

"So whose is it?" Karen asked.

"Beats me," Zeke admitted.

"Look at these footprints in the dust," Jen said.

She aimed her flashlight beyond the spot where they were standing.

"Those are mine," Karen said, pointing.

"But those aren't." Jen kept the light steady on a pair of larger footprints. "And there are Slinky's paw prints. Hey, what's that?" Something small and round sparkled in the dim light. Jen picked up the object and turned it over in her hand.

Zeke peered closely at it. "Weird. It's a button."

Karen stared at the sparkling sphere without saying anything.

"It's definitely a clue," Jen said, slipping the button into her pocket. "Someone came down here and lost it!"

Zeke held up three fingers. "So now we have the pick, the footprints, and the button."

"Come on," Karen said hastily as her flashlight flickered. "Let's get out of here. I think my flashlight is about to go dead."

The group hurried back along the tunnel and up the thirty steps to the short hall where the door into the pantry was still open.

"There's a door on that side, too," Karen explained, pointing to the opposite wall.

"From the parlor," said Jen. "That's how you

disappeared last night." Jen grinned. "We thought you were a ghost."

Karen smiled. "Maybe I am."

As soon as they stepped into the pantry, Zeke pulled the hidden door closed and an entire panel of shelves clicked back into place. It was completely camouflaged. If a person didn't know it was there, no way would he find it. They were on their way to the parlor to talk when Mrs. Mills pounced on them. Her raincoat was still zipped and water droplets glistened on the lavender fabric.

"There you are, Karen," she said. "I found the cutest store in town. I came all the way back here to drag you down there. We can get souvenirs. Come on."

Karen looked at the twins and shrugged. "Later, you guys."

Jen and Zeke nodded. They knew what she meant by *later*. Later they would try to sort out the clues and find the treasure.

The twins peeked into the parlor where Mrs. Snyder was sitting in the corner chair, thumbing through a book. Not wanting to disturb her or be over-heard, they settled into the two comfortable window chairs in the foyer.

"So if everyone here knows about the treasure and is probably interested in it," Zeke said quietly, "that means the pick could belong to any one of the guests."

Jen nodded glumly. "That doesn't help us at all."

"The footprints were pretty big so they probably belong to a man—Professor Snyder or Jaspar."

"But they were smudged, so they could actually belong to anyone."

Zeke frowned. "True. And we have a button with no idea of who lost it."

"The best we can do, then, is try to solve Catherine's riddle. Since Karen is the only person with the diary, we have a clue no one else has."

"*As always,*" Zeke recited, "*X marks the spot to the left.*"

"That's a big help," Jen said. "It sounds like something from a really bad pirate movie. 'X marks the spot to the left.'" They lounged around for the next hour, cozy in the chairs, when suddenly Jen bolted upright in her seat.

"What?" Zeke asked, sensing his sister's excitement.

Jen grabbed his arm. "Come on!" She raced through the parlor and into the small bathroom. Mrs. Snyder started to say something, but Jen quickly shut the door.

In a strained whisper, Jen said, "When we were refinishing the parlor and the bathroom a couple of years ago, I noticed something. Aunt Bee said to leave it because this wall is obviously part of the original old building." She pointed to the scarred wall behind the sink. "She thought it would add a little old-time charm. So," Jen continued more slowly as she lifted off the mirror from above the sink. "Look at this."

Zeke stared at a cross carved into the wall. It had been hidden by the hanging mirror. "What does a crooked cross have to do with anything?"

Jen widened her eyes at her brother. She tilted her head to the left. "Look at it like this!"

Zeke followed her example. *"As always, X marks the spot to the left!"* With his head tilted to the left, the crooked cross became a clear X on the wall. "And look." He pointed. Just to the left of the X was a knothole in the old wood. It, too, had been covered by the mirror. Zeke pulled his Swiss army knife out of his pocket. Very carefully, he prodded at the knothole. It didn't budge.

"Dig at it more," Jen suggested.

Zeke stuck the shiny blade of his knife along one edge of the hole. He pushed it in deeper. Then, very carefully, he twisted the knife.

"It moved!" Jen exclaimed.

Trying not to scratch the wall any more than necessary, Zeke pried his knife loose and the knothole popped out like a cork.

The twins peered into the small cavity left behind. Jen stuck two fingers into the hole and removed a folded yellowed piece of paper.

The Ghost of the Dark Lighthouse

Suddenly someone banged on the door. "What's going on in there?" called a voice. "Are you okay?"

Jen hastily hung up the mirror to cover the X and the hole in the wall. "It's Mrs. Snyder. Let's go."

Zeke opened the door and the twins stepped out. "We're fine," he said. "Just, uh, tightening up the bolts on the cabinet. It's all nice and sturdy now."

"Oh," Mrs. Snyder said, narrowing her eyes.

The twins were saved from any further questions by the arrival of Karen and her mother.

Jen grinned at Karen. "We were just about to play Monopoly. Want to come?"

"Monopoly?" Karen said, wrinkling her forehead. Zeke gave her a look.

"Oh!" Karen turned to her mother. "Can I go with them?"

Mrs. Mills sighed. "Fine, go have fun." She gave

Karen a hug and headed for the dining room, where Aunt Bee had left thermoses of hot coffee and cocoa and several mugs.

Karen followed Jen and Zeke through the foyer, down the hall, and around the corner.

"Wait till you see what we found," Zeke exclaimed as soon as they were out of sight near the back stairs, trying to keep his voice down.

Karen's eyes widened. "You found the treasure already?"

Jen giggled under her breath. "Not yet, but we may have found something." She carefully handed over the old, brittle piece of paper and explained where they had found it.

Her fingers trembling with excitement, Karen unfolded it. First she read it silently. Her face fell. *"When Christmas goes, it leaves behind what I know."*

Jen made a face. "Why can't it just say to look under the third floorboard in the foyer to find the gold?"

"When Christmas goes, it leaves behind what I know," Zeke repeated, nodding thoughtfully.

"What was that?" Karen suddenly whispered. "I just heard a creak, like a squeaky floorboard."

Zeke cocked his head to listen, but could only hear Mrs. Snyder coughing in the parlor and the storm steadily blowing against the B&B.

Jen tiptoed around the corner, but the hall was clear all the way into the foyer. "Nothing. Maybe it was the Ghost of the Dark Lighthouse."

"What are you talking about?" Zeke demanded.

"There's been so much talk of ghosts and dark lighthouses," Jen replied, "I thought I'd give her a name."

Karen saw the twins were just kidding around, and her shoulders eased. "I thought you were serious."

Jen laughed. "Oh, we've heard ghostly noises before, but I don't think there's anything to worry about."

Even so, all three of them were alert on their way upstairs to Karen's room, the Sunflower Studio. They'd decided she should hide the note there before they continued their search for the treasure. After looking around, Karen tucked the note far under the dresser. Then they made their way downstairs again.

"Let's ask Aunt Bee if she knows anything about the treasure," Zeke suggested.

"But you said you wouldn't tell anyone," Karen said, a look of panic on her face.

Jen patted her arm. "Don't worry. We won't tell her anything important. Besides, if Aunt Bee really thought there was a treasure hidden here somewhere, she'd probably help us hunt for it."

They looked for her in the parlor, but found only

Mrs. Snyder. "There you are. Tell me what you were *really* doing in the bathroom," Mrs. Snyder demanded.

But before they had to make up an excuse, someone dropped a heavy object somewhere in the B&B. Suddenly, Mrs. Snyder broke into one of her coughing and sneezing fits. At one point she sneezed with such force, her purse flew off her lap.

Trying not to laugh, Jen quickly picked it up for her. She wasn't prepared for the weight of the purse, and it slipped sideways in her hand, spilling a few items.

"Sorry," she apologized, handing Mrs. Snyder the large red bag and picking up a packet of tissues, a key chain, and a book. Jen turned over the book and just had time to glance at the cover before Mrs. Snyder snatched it out of her hand.

Mrs. Snyder shoved the book back into her purse. She immediately started blowing her nose again.

Jen figured this was a good time to escape, so with a quick good-bye, she led the others out of the parlor. As soon as they were out of earshot, she whispered, "Did you guys see the title of that book? It was something about searching for treasure. Do you think she's the one hunting in the tunnels?"

"Mrs. Snyder hangs out in the parlor all the time. When would she have time to hunt?" Zeke asked.

"We'd hear her blowing her nose in the tunnels,

for sure," Karen added with a giggle. "I noticed that sound carries easily from the B&B into the tunnels."

They found Aunt Bee painting on a large canvas in her room. So far the painting looked like globs of red, orange, and purple. But Jen knew her aunt would transform it into a vivid sunset or beautiful close-up of a flower by the time she was through.

"Oh, sure," Aunt Bee said, after Zeke explained what they wanted. "There are rumors of treasure in many small towns. But I've never found evidence to support the rumors here in Mystic."

"Where can we find out more?" Jen asked.

Aunt Bee thought a moment. "There's an old book called *A Villager's Thoughts on a Small Town*, which is all about Mystic in the old days. That's the only place I've seen any treasure mentioned in writing. Happy hunting," she called as they left.

"We should go to the library and check out that book. Maybe it'll give us a hint about the Christmas clue," Jen said doubtfully. "At least we'll get out of the house."

On the way to the front door, they spotted Esther behind the registration desk. When she saw them, she straightened abruptly, a blush of red staining her cheeks. Patting her hair, she said, "You startled me. I was looking for a pen."

Jen reached over and plucked one from a cup full of pens on top of the counter and handed it to her.

"Oh, thank you. I didn't see those there." The pen in one hand and a lantern in the other, she hurried off.

None of them was looking forward to sloshing through the cold rain, but once they were outside and walking briskly, it wasn't too bad. Zeke, of course, didn't really mind getting wet. Sailing and swimming were two of his favorite activities, but stomping through puddles wasn't quite the same.

About twenty minutes and several shortcuts later, as they were nearing the library in town, Karen nudged Jen. "Don't look now," she said under her breath, "but I think there's someone following us."

Jen casually stopped to look in a window at a display of shoes and glanced behind them. There was someone! It looked like a man, but she couldn't be sure without staring, and she didn't want to be too obvious. As they continued on their way, Jen glanced behind them every once in a while. The person in the gray raincoat was still tailing them.

They hurried on to the library, and when Jen checked behind them one last time before they went in, there was the gray figure, standing across the street pretending to tie a shoe. Shaking off a chill, she followed Zeke and Karen into the library.

They hunted the stacks for the book Aunt Bee had told them about. They finally found it in a distant corner.

"I don't think anyone's ever taken this book out," Karen said, sneezing from the dust.

Handling the old, musty book with his fingertips, Zeke flipped through it. It didn't take him long to find the passage about treasure. "This is all it says: *Unto this day, the rumor persists of a ghost who blows out the lanterns in the lighthouse tower. In the black of night, without the light to guide them safely, ships wreck upon the rocks, leaving their treasures to the hungry ocean. The rumor would have one believe that the Ghost of the Dark Lighthouse reaped the treasure from the sea and hid it somewhere in the lighthouse.*"

"So there *is* something known as the Ghost of the Dark Lighthouse," Jen said.

"And the treasure from all the shipwrecks must be somewhere," Zeke muttered, closing the book and replacing it on the shelf.

On the return walk, Jen kept a sharp lookout but never saw any sign of anyone following them. They got back to the B&B, toweled off, and headed to the dining room for some hot cocoa. As they sipped their drinks and munched on cookies, Zeke reviewed the clues they had already found. Finally, he said, "If only we could figure out the Christmas clue, maybe we'd have some answers."

Jen plunked some marshmallows into her mug. "I wonder what Christmas was like back then."

"Catherine never wrote much about it in her diary," Karen offered. She took a sip of cocoa. "She always made gifts for her parents, and they each gave her one present."

"Like the teddy bear in that old photo," Jen said absently. "I bet that was a Christmas gift."

Zeke snapped his fingers. "That's it!"

9

Stolen

"What's 'it'?" Jen asked.

"The Christmas photo. Come on, I have an idea."
He raced into the museum, with Jen and Karen right
behind him. *"When Christmas goes, it leaves behind
what I know.* This is a long shot, but it's worth a try."
He carefully lifted the silver-framed photograph of
Catherine Markham off the wall and turned it over.
The back of the photograph was covered with a piece
of paper. Zeke carefully removed it and revealed two
lines of writing on the back of the picture.
Triumphantly, he showed it to them.

One line read: *Catherine—Christmas 1901.* The
next line, written in different handwriting, read:
When the lighthouse is dark, the distant shore is the mark.

"Another clue!" Karen exclaimed. "That's definitely Catherine's handwriting."

Zeke put the protective piece of paper back in place and rehung the picture on the wall. "I think we need to look at everything we've found so far. Let's look at all the clues and see if there's anything we missed."

"How will it help to look at the first clue when we already found the next one?" Jen asked.

"Maybe there was something else written on the note that we missed."

"Or something written on the back," Karen said, agreeing with Zeke.

Jen thought they were being too hopeful—after all, she had studied the note carefully—but she knew it'd be no use arguing with them. She followed them up the stairs to the Sunflower Studio, where Karen had hidden the paper.

Karen opened the door to her room and gasped. "Oh, no!"

Zeke looked around at the mess. The beds were completely unmade and clothes lay scattered all around. All the drawers in the dresser stood open. Nothing looked broken or damaged in any way, but it would still take some time to straighten up. Obviously someone had been looking for something—probably Catherine's diary. Since Mrs. Mills had mentioned the diary and the treasure together, someone must have thought they'd be able to find the treasure if they had the diary. Luckily, Karen had left the diary at home.

"Your mom didn't do this, right?" Zeke asked, just to be sure.

Karen looked at him as if he were crazy. "No way. She hasn't seen this yet or we would have heard her yelling. And if I don't hurry and clean it up, she'll know we're up to something. Then she'll make me tell her what's going on."

"Then we'd better clean it up before she gets back," Zeke said.

Working together at top speed, it only took the three of them a few minutes to sort through the mess and put everything back in order. Finally finished, the twins settled on the edge of the bed while Karen poked under the dresser for the paper she'd hidden there, which was why they'd come up here in the first place. Then she lay her face sideways on the floor and stared under the piece of furniture.

"It's gone!"

"What?" Zeke exclaimed, getting on his hands and knees to look. Sure enough, the paper was gone. So the person had found the clue instead of the diary—but the clue was even more important. He jumped to his feet. "The second clue!" He ran all the way to the museum and Jen and Karen followed not far behind.

They whipped into the museum and stumbled to a halt in front of the space where the Christmas photograph had hung just moments before. The photograph was gone!

10

Help Me!

"Someone stole the clues right out from under our noses," Karen said hoarsely.

"That means someone is watching every move we make," Jen said, warily looking around. "They're figuring out the clues just after we are. But maybe now they're ahead of us and they'll find the treasure first."

Aunt Bee popped her head through the doorway. "Time to get lunch ready!"

Zeke pointed to the empty spot on the wall. "One of the old photos is missing," he told his aunt.

Aunt Bee frowned. "How strange." Then she brightened. "But I'm sure it'll show up. Surely there are no thieves here."

Zeke looked at the two girls with raised eyebrows. The twins knew they couldn't tell Aunt Bee everything that was going on because she'd tell them not to get involved. But they were sure one of their guests *was* a thief. And if they didn't stop that person, the treasure would be stolen, too.

Jen stepped forward and wiped a smudge of bright red oil paint from Aunt Bee's cheek. "I'm sure the photo will turn up," Jen said, agreeing with her aunt. "I'm starving. Let's eat!"

Aunt Bee didn't say another word about the photograph of Catherine Markham as they helped her lay out the ingredients for a sandwich buffet. Karen also helped, even though Jen and Zeke told her she didn't have to. She was supposed to be on vacation.

"If I sit around, I'll just worry," Karen reasoned, sticking a knife in the mustard.

Just as they were getting ready to eat, Detective Wilson drove up and let himself inside. "What good timing," he joked.

Jen and Zeke grinned. He always had good timing when it came to eating Aunt Bee's food. Even with the electricity off, she made fantastic meals, and Detective Wilson knew it.

Jen thought the retired detective had a crush on Aunt Bee. He was always stopping by to help with repairs around the B&B. One of her fresh-from-the-oven muffins or a slice of blueberry pie was always the perfect reward once the repair was finished.

When all the guests were sitting down to their overstuffed sandwiches of ham, turkey, or roast beef, Aunt Bee called for everyone's attention. She introduced Detective Wilson, explaining that he would fill their sinks with water so that they could wash up after lunch.

Jen shivered. Washing up in freezing-cold water didn't sound that great. She'd rather wait till the electricity came back on. After all, it was not usually out for more than two days.

"It has been brought to my attention," Aunt Bee continued, "that a photograph from the museum is missing. We do have a mischievous ghost living here who probably moved it as a joke, so if any of you find it, would you please return it?"

After they finished eating, Aunt Bee agreed to give Professor Snyder and Jaspar a "quick and wet" tour of the town.

"I'll just stay here and knit," Mrs. Snyder said when her husband asked if she'd like to join them.

"What are you going to do?" Karen asked her mom.

Mrs. Mills yawned and stretched. "Oooh, I think I'll take a nap. It's perfect napping weather."

After the dining room emptied out, Jen and Zeke cleared the table and prepared to wash the dishes.

"I guess I'll go exploring," Karen said when the twins insisted that she shouldn't help them. "Come find me when you're done."

Zeke nodded. "Don't forget a flashlight," he called after her, knowing she would need it if the storm made the sky any darker.

She held one up, switched it on, and headed for the foyer.

Jen and Zeke hurried through the kitchen chores. They knew they would have to clean the guests' rooms later, but they were hoping that if they finished quickly in the kitchen, they'd have some time for treasure hunting.

As they finished the dishes, Detective Wilson picked up an empty bucket. "I'm going to start filling up everyone's sinks," the retired detective told the twins.

"Do you want us to get our raincoats and help you carry water in from the well?" Zeke asked.

Detective Wilson shook his head. "No, no, I can handle this job myself."

"But—" Zeke tried to interrupt.

Detective Wilson winked. "The more I do, the bigger my payment."

"You mean the bigger the slice of pie you get," Jen said, laughing.

"You've got me pretty well figured out," Detective

Wilson chuckled. He headed outside with the empty bucket and the twins took off before he could change his mind.

"We should find Karen," Zeke said as they were walking into the foyer. "Maybe she found another clue."

Jen agreed and they combed the first floor looking for their friend.

They couldn't find her anywhere downstairs, so they headed up the front staircase. Zeke frowned. "I get the feeling something's not right."

"Do you think she's investigating the tunnels?" asked Jen.

"Maybe," Zeke replied. "But I don't think she'd go without us, now that we're all working together."

Upstairs, they softly called Karen's name.

Zeke stopped. "Did you hear that?"

"Karen?" Jen repeated.

A muffled thump came from somewhere around the corner. The twins tiptoed forward. They peeked down the side hall. Nothing.

"Karen?" Jen called again.

The thump sounded louder.

"It's coming from the hall linen closet," Zeke said, pointing to the closed door.

"Help me!" The distant voice coming from the closet was Karen's.

11
Mystery and Intrigue

Jen raced forward, hastily turning the old-fashioned key that still stuck out of the lock, and opened the door.

Karen fell out of the linen closet. "I thought you'd never find me," she gasped. Her face was as pale as one of the extra sheets they kept in the closet.

"What happened?"

"I don't really know. I was just looking around up here when I heard a door open somewhere behind me. But before I could turn around, someone shoved me into the closet and locked the door! I was squeezed in there so tight with all the sheets, I felt like a mummy."

"How long were you in there?" Jen asked.

"I don't know. It was probably only a few minutes. Did you pass anyone in the hall?"

Jen shook her head.

Zeke flashed a light on his watch. "We'd better

get to the cleaning. Aunt Bee will be home soon and she'll expect us to have the rooms done."

"I'm coming with you this time," Karen said. "No way am I going to be locked up again. I could have suffocated in there."

The twins retrieved the cleaning supplies from the kitchen and started downstairs with the Snyders' room, the Violet Valley, since they knew the professor was in town and Mrs. Snyder was knitting in the parlor.

"Yuck!" Jen exclaimed. "Look at those disgusting socks. And I thought *your* socks were dirty," she said to her brother.

"Very funny," Zeke said. He liked to take off his shoes and wear socks around the house so his feet wouldn't get cold, which made them dirtier than usual. But these socks looked as if the professor had worn them *outside* without shoes on.

"I'll just sweep them into a corner," Jen said, making a face. "No way am I touching them."

Other than the socks, the Snyders' room was fairly neat. The Professor had three tall stacks of books piled on the dresser and the small bedside table, but at least they weren't thrown all over the room.

"Look at this," Zeke said suddenly. He pointed to one of the books in the highest stack.

Jen walked over with the broom in her hands and tipped her head sideways. *"A Villager's Thoughts on a Small Town.* Hey, that's the book we looked at in the library!"

Zeke carefully examined the binding. "The same book, but not the same copy. This book must belong to the professor because it doesn't have a library label on it."

"Well, he *is* writing a book on Maine," Karen reasoned. "All these other books of his are about small towns in Maine, too."

Jen returned to sweeping. The broom bristles hit something under the bed. Gingerly, she moved the broom so that she could drag the object out of the shadows. In the dim light, she wasn't sure she was seeing the object correctly. She bent down for a closer look.

"You guys!" she exclaimed, picking up the framed photograph. "It's Catherine Markham!"

"How did it get in here?" Zeke demanded.

"I don't know. The Snyders must have taken it," Jen said, gripping the photo in one hand and the broom in the other.

"There's no way to tell who the real thief is without asking them," Zeke said.

"But then they'll know we're up to something," Karen said, panic in her voice. "And they might say something to my mom."

Jen nodded in agreement. "We can't let anyone know about this. Let's just leave it here and see what happens."

No one else could think of anything better to do with the photo, so they agreed. Jen gently slipped it back under the bed.

Next they moved upstairs to the Sunflower Studio. They tapped softly on the door. If Mrs. Mills was asleep already, they didn't want to wake her. When there was no answer, Karen silently opened the door and peeked in.

"She's not here!" Karen exclaimed. She opened

the door a little wider.

"Maybe she couldn't sleep," Jen suggested.

Karen shrugged. "Maybe. But anyway, our room is already neat, thanks to whoever messed it up before."

"Still," Jen said, heading for the bathroom with a bucket and sponge, "we'd better clean. It'll only take a sec."

When they were done, they trudged through the hall to the Rose Room. When they knocked on Esther's door, she called, "Just a minute." She finally opened the door, her head wrapped up in a towel turban. "I was just washing my hair."

"In freezing-cold water?" Jen asked.

"That's right," Esther said. "It was so cold it gave me quite a headache. But at least I have clean hair now."

Jen shivered, imagining the frigid water on her scalp. She'd rather go with dirty hair for an extra day than freeze her brain like that.

"You kids must love living here," Esther said cheerily.

"It's pretty cool," Zeke admitted.

"Imagine having a treasure hidden right here."

Jen and Zeke looked at each other.

"Sure," Jen said. "But we don't know if there really is a treasure. It's probably just a rumor."

"But what if it's true?" Esther went on. "You could

have a real treasure hunt. So much mystery and intrigue!"

The entire time they were in her room, Esther talked and asked questions about life at the B&B, but every other question seemed to refer to the hidden treasure.

After a while, Jen stopped answering, letting Zeke do all the talking. She was afraid she'd let something slip out about the tunnels or the clues.

She breathed a sigh of relief when they finished cleaning and were able to leave. "Esther sure is nosy," she said under her breath.

"Not only that," Zeke said urgently, "but did you see the miniature tape recorder she had on her dresser?"

Jen and Karen shook their heads.

"It was hidden behind the clock. And it was *on* the whole time. She was recording our conversation!"

As they tried to figure out why she was recording what they said, they headed for Jaspar's room. He was still in town, so they quickly swept and dusted, eager to get back to their treasure hunt.

Karen pushed a couple of dresser drawers to close them. "Hey, this drawer is stuck," she said.

Zeke tried to push it in. "That's weird. Something must be jammed in it."

Jen and Karen watched as Zeke pulled the drawer

open before he tried to close it again.

"Look!" Jen exclaimed as something in the drawer caught her eye. "There's a book wedged in there crooked. Look at what it is!"

The three of them stared in amazement at the exact book they had looked at in the library that morning. And this time it wasn't a copy of the book, it was the *same* book. A Mystic Public Library label glowed up at them.

"So he was the one following us," Jen breathed. "He must be trying to find the treasure."

Karen clutched Jen's arm. "Do you think he locked me in the closet?"

"Impossible," Zeke said. "Remember, he's in town with Aunt Bee and Professor Snyder."

"Does that mean there's more than one person after the treasure?" Karen asked.

"Everyone heard about it from your mother," Jen pointed out. "For all we know, *everyone* is hunting for it!"

They headed downstairs to dust the parlor before they put away the cleaning supplies. Mrs. Snyder and Esther were talking.

Zeke nudged Jen and whispered. "Look at Esther. Notice anything strange?"

Jen stared. "Her hair is dry! How could it be dry if she just washed it? There's no electricity for a blow-dryer."

"Exactly."

Suddenly Mrs. Snyder started sneezing and coughing. Zeke pricked up his ears. He could have sworn he heard something, but now all he could hear was Mrs. Snyder blowing her nose. But when the woman took a breath between blows, an eerie wailing filled the room.

12

Trapped

The spooky noise sent shivers down to Jen's toes.

Esther's face suddenly grew pale. "The ghost!" she cried out.

Mrs. Snyder looked worried. But before she could comment, she erupted into another sneezing attack. She dug through her handbag for more tissues, mumbling that she didn't know her husband had returned from town.

"Come on," Zeke said, leaving the parlor. When they were out of earshot he turned to the girls. "That's not a ghost. The sound is coming from the tunnels."

They hurried to the pantry. The secret door was open just a crack, and the strange wailing sound was actually wind whistling through the narrow slit. Zeke opened the door a bit wider and the sound stopped.

Jen grabbed a flashlight and started down the

stairs. "Someone's down there. Let's go!"

"Wait," Zeke called, but Jen kept going. She knew that the only way they'd solve this mystery was to find out who else knew about these tunnels. And the only way to do that was to catch the person right now.

Jen turned on her flashlight and thumped down the stairs, following what she thought were footsteps ahead of her. Zeke and Karen raced after her, but Jen's years on the soccer team had given her extra quickness on her feet. At the foot of the stairs she stopped and held her breath, listening. She waited for Zeke and Karen to catch up.

"I lost him," she said with regret.

Zeke looked around in the dim light. "Hey, what's that?" he said, pointing off to the right into a little nook Jen hadn't noticed before. In the shadowed light it looked like a crouching animal.

They inched forward. Jen jabbed at it with the tip of her shoe, but nothing sprang up at her or bit off her foot. She leaned closer. "It's just dusty clothes," she said finally, "and a pair of boots."

"Why are they down here?"

"Maybe so whoever is hunting for the treasure won't get their regular clothes and shoes dirty. If that person always has clean clothes and shoes, we might never guess he or she has been down here."

"Their feet sure would get dirty on their way to the boots, though," Karen commented. "Just think—"

A creak of wood sounded from the tunnel leading up to the left.

Jen motioned up the set of stairs. "Someone went that way," she whispered. "Where does that tunnel lead?" she asked Karen.

"It goes up to another secret door in one of the guest rooms."

They made their way stealthily up the steps and then down a long tunnel. At the end, the passage turned sharply, revealing another set of stairs. But by the time they got to the top, the tunnel was empty. Whoever it was had exited through a secret door into the Daffodil Den, which was empty this week, and disappeared.

"The only person it could have been," Zeke said when he caught his breath, "was Mrs. Mills." He looked at Karen apologetically.

"It couldn't have been my mother," Karen insisted quickly. "She doesn't care about treasure. Besides, she thinks it's all a big story anyway."

"Maybe we should just see if she's in your room," Zeke suggested.

They trooped to the door of the Sunflower Studio and rapped on it politely. No one answered. They were about to turn and leave when the door opened.

"Hi, kids," Mrs. Mills said. "I thought I heard something. Were you knocking on my door?"

"Yeah," Karen said quickly. "I was looking for you a little while ago. Where were you, Mom?"

Mrs. Mills held up a paperback book. "I was borrowing this from the parlor."

"We didn't see you down there," Zeke said.

"You must have just missed me." Mrs. Mills retreated into her room and flopped back onto the bed. "When I couldn't nap, I decided I'd read. Was there something you wanted, honey?"

Jen heard several male voices coming from downstairs. Aunt Bee, Jaspar, and the Professor had returned. She turned to Karen. "We'll see you later. Try to find out what's going on," she added in a whisper.

Karen nodded and closed the door between them.

On the way downstairs, Jen stopped Zeke on the middle step. "Did you notice?"

Zeke nodded glumly. "How could I miss it? Mrs. Mills's shoes were dusty and smudged just like ours. She must have been in the tunnels."

"Not only that," Jen added, "she was missing a button on her sweater. A sparkly round button that matched the one we found in the tunnel!"

They started down the stairs again. "That means

Mrs. Mills is definitely after the treasure. But does Karen know?"

"Maybe, maybe not. Let's just keep an eye on her. I like Karen and I don't want to hurt her feelings by accusing her mother of lying to us."

By dinnertime the storm was starting to clear. Electricity still hadn't been restored to the B&B, but Aunt Bee guessed it was only a matter of hours before they'd have power again. The guests all cheered.

"Though I do love eating by candlelight," Esther gushed.

"I prefer electricity," Jaspar grumbled. But he couldn't keep a sour face for long and grinned.

"Why are you so happy?" Professor Snyder asked.

"Well, I really shouldn't tell you," Jaspar admitted. "My next live television special has been approved."

"What is it?" Jen asked.

"I really can't tell you." He winked. "It's a big secret."

Jen's stomach squeezed uncomfortably. *Could his special have anything to do with the hidden treasure?* She glanced at Zeke and then Karen. They were obviously all thinking the same thing.

The three of them soon excused themselves, promising Aunt Bee they would do the dishes later. They headed into the foyer where no one could hear them.

"Jaspar must be after the treasure," Karen wailed. "He's going to ruin everything. I just know Catherine Markham would hate her treasure to be on TV."

"Then there's only one thing to do," Jen said, agreeing with Karen. "We have to find it first!"

"But we haven't figured out the last clue," Zeke said.

"We don't have time for that now," Jen insisted. "The most obvious place for the treasure to be hidden is in the tunnels. We'll just have to dig around till we find it. As soon as everyone goes to bed, we have to go down there."

It wasn't until eleven that Zeke felt confident that everyone had settled down for the night. The twins met Karen in the parlor just as the clock was striking eleven-fifteen.

"Ready?" Zeke whispered.

"Did you bring your flashlight?" Jen asked her brother. The tunnels were always pitch-black, but going down there late at night was somehow spookier.

"I couldn't find it."

"Me neither."

"Someone doesn't want us snooping around!"

"We'll have to use a lantern," Jen said, taking the

one that sat on the foyer counter. She lit it carefully. The light wavered as they made their way through the silent B&B to the secret door in the parlor.

Taking a deep breath, Jen said, "I'll go first since I'm holding the light." No one argued with her.

It seemed to take forever to descend the thirty steps. At last they reached the rocky floor of the tunnel. They were huddled together and the feeble light from the lantern didn't reach very far.

"See anything yet?" Karen whispered.

"The clothes are missing," Jen hissed.

They all looked at the shallow alcove where they had last seen the pile of clothes and the boots. The space was bare.

"Not even a single clue," Zeke said, frowning. "Let's go look in that storage room you mentioned. Maybe you missed something in there."

Keeping so close together made it hard to walk, but the three of them continued down the tunnel. At the three-way split, they turned off to the left. The path sloped down a bit, and before long they found themselves in a room carved out of the rock. It seemed to be as large as the parlor. As Karen had described, old, empty bookshelves leaned against the walls.

Jen opened her mouth to say something, but Zeke

held up his hand for quiet. An odd scraping sound filled the silence.

Jen felt like her ears were going to explode, she was listening so hard, but the sound had stopped.

Zeke motioned for them to walk quietly back to the main tunnel. Still holding the lantern, Jen knew she'd have to go first. Dread weighed down her feet. Each step was a chore. All she wanted to do was hide in a corner. *Are we crazy to be down here in the middle of the night?* But even as this thought ran through her head, she put one foot in front of the other.

The light in the lantern flickered in a sudden breeze. Jen moved her hand up to block the light wind. Too late! The light blew out, leaving them in complete darkness.

13

The Key

Karen let out a little squeak, but it sounded more like a rusty hinge than anything human.

Someone tugged on Jen's arm and she nearly dropped the dark lantern.

"Shhhhh," Zeke hissed.

Jen bit her tongue to keep from shouting. She felt totally lost. Which way was out? Then she heard the scraping sound again. Or was it a dragging sound?

Zeke felt Karen tense beside him. Suddenly, she erupted into a fit of sneezing. The dust!

The odd sound stopped. Then, a huge shape pushed past them. The kids were scattered in the narrow tunnel like bowling pins. Whoever it was held a dim flashlight, and Jen caught a glimpse of dusty clothes and heavy boots.

"Hey!" Zeke shouted, but the soft sound of

running feet didn't stop. A few seconds later there was complete silence—and total darkness again.

"Is everyone okay?" he whispered, worried that the intruder might still be lurking in the tunnels.

"I'm okay," Jen said. Her voice sounded a bit shaky.

"Me, too," Karen said from off to the left. "Who was that?"

Jen said, "Whoever he was—"

"Or she," Zeke interrupted.

"—has some explaining to do. I nearly cracked my skull open on the wall."

"I didn't hear the lantern break."

Jen grinned in the darkness. "I might have broken my head, but I saved the lamp."

"Let's get out of here," Karen said.

"Let's go this way," Zeke said. "This is the way the intruder went, so it must be the way out."

In the inky blackness, Jen grabbed a piece of Zeke's shirt with one hand. Behind her, Karen did the same to her shirt. Attached like a train, the three of them slowly chugged their way down the passage. At last they rounded a bend and Zeke nearly tripped over the first step up. Even though he knew they were finally close to getting out of the tunnels, his heart didn't stop hammering until they reached the top of the stairs.

Breathing a huge sigh of relief, they stepped out of

the passage and closed the secret door behind them. Shafts of light from the full moon were streaming into the parlor, giving them enough light to see. They seemed like spotlights to Jen after the complete blackness of the tunnels.

"Let's go up to my room to talk," Zeke whispered.

They made their way silently to the still-dark lighthouse tower and climbed the circular stairs up to Zeke's room.

"Cool," Karen said, examining his room by moonlight. She moved to a window. "Wow, great view."

Jen and Zeke crowded behind her to look out. "There's an even better view from the observation platform on the top," Zeke said. "But the lighthouse lamp is so bright that it's hard to get a good view at night. During the day the view is great."

"We could go see the view now," Jen commented. "The lighthouse is dark because we still don't have electricity."

Zeke snapped his fingers. "That's it!"

"What's it?" Karen asked, turning away from the window.

Zeke didn't answer. All he said was, "Come on!"

He dashed for the stairs that led up to the platform. The metal circular stairs rang with each hurried footstep, echoing all the way down the stairwell. They burst through the door onto the observation deck.

The view was breathtaking. The moon had sneaked out from behind a storm cloud and scattered moonlight gleamed like quicksilver on the Atlantic Ocean. Although the storm had started to clear, the water was still rough, and it whipped and crashed on the rocks far below them. For a long moment, no one spoke.

Finally Zeke said, "Okay, what do you see?"

"The ocean," Karen said, sounding doubtful. "But so what?"

Zeke huffed with impatience. "What else do you see?"

"The rocks below, the roof of the house," Jen answered.

"The bay," Karen added. "Clouds."

Jen put her hand on Karen's arm to stop her. She peered through the night. Sure enough, there was the bay. Beyond that she could just make out—"The distant shore!" she exclaimed.

"Exactly!" exclaimed Zeke.

"When the lighthouse is dark," Karen recited from memory, "the distant shore is the mark."

"The clue," Jen said. "It must lead up here."

"Catherine Markham must have hidden a clue up here that can only be found when the lighthouse is dark," said Zeke. "When the light is on, it is too bright up here to see the distant shore."

"But they didn't have electricity back then," Karen said, sounding confused. "Professor Snyder said that the lighthouse keeper filled the oil lamps twice a night to keep the light burning, so why would it ever be dark?"

"Maybe if he got too sick," Jen said. "Then maybe the lighthouse did go dark."

"Let's look along the side of the lighthouse that faces the distant shore," Zeke said, already crouching down to examine the stone wall that circled the platform. The three of them hunted in silence.

Jen leaned over the wall, trying not to notice how far down the rocks were. With her heart in her throat, she was about to give up her search when a glimmer of something caught her eye. But when she looked again, the glimmer was gone. Figuring it must have been a figment of her imagination, she was about to turn away when the moon broke through a hazy cloud. The shimmering globe illuminated everything so brightly that the night suddenly seemed to be day.

Jen took one more look over the edge of the wall. Yes! There was something shiny between two stone blocks that seemed to pick up the light of the moon and glow with a blue hue. It was just within reach. She pulled. It came loose in her fingers. With a cry of dismay, Jen felt it drop free and plunge out of sight.

Zeke and Karen gathered on either side of her. "What happened?"

Karen gulped and moved away from the wall. "That is way scary," she said.

"I saw something shine in the moonlight. But when I dug it out, it fell out of my hand. I think I lost the clue!" She leaned over the wall and poked her fingers in the hole left by the missing rock. "Wait a minute. I didn't," she said triumphantly. "I found the clue!" She

stood back, clutching something in her hand. She gave it to Karen. "It's your treasure hunt, so you look at it."

Karen carefully unfolded the old piece of paper. "It's oil paper," she said. "It's what they used to use to keep things dry before they had plastic wrap and waxed paper. But now it's old and crumbly."

The paper fell away to reveal another folded paper. When Karen carefully unfolded that one, they were amazed to see an old-fashioned key.

"That looks like the old key in the upstairs linen closet," Jen said. "What's it for?"

Karen shook her head. "Listen to this." She began reading. "*I, Jacob Markham*—that was Catherine's father," she added, "*do hereby swear to keep the lighthouse lamp burning from this day forth until the day I die.*"

"I thought that was his job," Jen interrupted.

"*No more will I purposely let the lamp go out so that ships will be lost and crash upon the shore.*"

The three of them gasped.

"*No more will I purposely lead ships onto the rocks with a lantern burning too far inland. No more will I steal from the wreckage nor collect the wealth the waves leave at my cruel hand. I will repent of the murders I have caused, now and forevermore.*"

14

Missing Clues

"I can't believe it," Jen finally breathed. "There wasn't a Ghost of the Dark Lighthouse. It was the keeper himself who let the lighthouse go dark!"

The three of them peeked over the wall, imagining the ships smashing onto the rocks far below. They hadn't crashed accidentally, but because Catherine's father had purposely led them onto the rocks so he could steal from the wrecked ships.

"How awful," Karen said.

"Catherine must have figured out what her father was doing and made him promise to stop," Zeke said. "And if he did it again, she'd use this confession against him."

Karen gulped. "I wonder what happened to her. Her diary ends the very same day this letter was written," she noted.

"What's the key for?" Jen asked.

"I don't know," Karen said, examining the key more closely. She handed it to Jen, then turned the letter over. "Hey, there's more." She turned the paper to catch the moonlight. "I can hardly read it. It seems to have some water damage or something. *I have hidden the treasures I stole . . .*"

"Where?" Jen exclaimed.

"It's all smudged. The only thing I can read is at the end where it says, *to use for a worthy cause.*"

"So there really *is* a treasure hidden somewhere," Zeke said. "That must be what the key is for."

"Now we just have to find it," Jen said.

"Unless someone else already has," Zeke said darkly. "Maybe that's the noise we heard in the tunnel tonight—someone dragging a treasure chest."

"And whoever it was didn't want to get caught," Karen said, rubbing her elbow where it had banged against the tunnel wall.

"But the thief won't have the key to open the treasure chest," Jen pointed out hopefully. "We just have to find where it's hidden and unlock it."

Jen handed the key back to Karen, who shivered. "But not tonight," Karen said. "I'm freezing, and my mom's going to worry about me if she notices I'm not in our room. We'll have to figure this out tomorrow morning. The treasure's safe as long as we have the key."

The three retraced their steps down the dark stairwell. Jen lit a lantern and walked Karen to her room so that she wouldn't bump into any of the furniture, then she returned to Zeke's room. She knew neither one of them would get any sleep until they talked about the mystery of the dark lighthouse.

Sure enough, Zeke was waiting for her. He'd lit a candle and already had sheets of paper in front of him. When she walked in with the lantern, he blew out the candle.

"It's time to fill out suspect sheets," he said. "It's the only way we'll figure out who else is searching for the treasure."

"All the guests look guilty to me. Even Mrs. Snyder, if you think about it."

Zeke raised his eyebrows. "How could she be guilty? All she does is sit in the parlor all day and sneeze."

"Exactly," Jen exclaimed. "Doesn't that seem a bit strange to you? And after all, the photograph *was* under her bed."

Zeke pondered that a second. "You're right," he said slowly. "But that doesn't make her guilty of pushing us over in the tunnels or leaving footprints in there."

Jen sighed. "True. But it must mean something."

Zeke picked up his pen. "Let's write down what we know."

Mystic Lighthouse

Suspect Sheet

Name: Esther Barr

Motive: Wants the treasure?

Clues: WHY IS SHE AVOIDING JASPAR?

Who was she talking to about the treasure? What did she mean when she said "do anything to get that treasure . . . whatever necessary to find it"?

SHE ASKED A LOT OF QUESTIONS ABOUT THE TREASURE, AND SHE IS TAPE RECORDING THE INFORMATION.

Why was she nosing around the B&B? She was looking for something on the check-in counter but said she was just looking for a pen, which was in plain view.

She couldn't have opened the secret passage door when we heard it moaning— she was in the parlor with Mrs. Snyder.

Why did she say she'd just washed her hair when she really hadn't? (Her hair was dry, but there was no electricity for a hair dryer!)

Mystic Lighthouse

Suspect Sheet

Name: Jaspar Westcombe

Motive: Professional investigative reporter and treasure hunter

Clues: He knows a lot about treasure and could have known about the lighthouse treasure before he came.

Who is he talking to on the phone all the time?

Why is he trying to talk to Esther, who keeps trying to avoid him?

Are those his footprints in the secret passageways?

Why did he follow us to the library?

Has book in room about the treasure and secret passages that he got from the library.

He has a new show he's excited about—could it be the lighthouse treasure?

Mystic Lighthouse

Suspect Sheet

Name: Professor Snyder

Motive: Wants to discover a part of history and wants the treasure

Clues: He admits he knows a lot about Mystic. He could have known about the treasure before he got here, also could know about the secret doors.

His suitcase was heavy—could he have been hiding tools in it?

Are those his footprints in the secret passage?

The Christmas photo was in his room.

But he wasn't at the B&B when the secret passage was opened to make that moaning sound.

Mystic Lighthouse

Suspect Sheet

Name: Mrs. Snyder

Motive: Wants the treasure for her husband?

Clues: KNOWS A LOT ABOUT MYSTIC THROUGH HER HUSBAND?

If she's really hard of hearing, why doesn't she wear a hearing aid? And why can she hear some things some of the time? Is she faking it?

She had a treasure-hunting book in her purse.

WHY WAS SHE SO INTERESTED WHEN WE WERE IN THE BATHROOM?

The Christmas photo was in her room.

She was in the parlor when the passage door was opened so she couldn't have done it.

Mystic Lighthouse

Suspect Sheet

Name: Lenore Mills

Motive: Wants the treasure?

Clues: SAYS THE TREASURE IS JUST A SILLY STORY, BUT MAYBE THAT'S JUST TO THROW OTHERS OFF THE TRACK.

PROBABLY KNOWS A LOT OF INFORMATION FROM HEARING IT FROM KAREN OVER THE YEARS.

Karen says she definitely knows about the secret passages because Karen told her all about them.

Her button was in the secret passage. Were her footprints in the tunnels?

SUPPOSEDLY TAKING A NAP, BUT WE COULDN'T FIND HER ANYWHERE.

Acted embarrassed when questioned about where she was when the secret passage door was opened.

SHE HAD DIRTY SHOES!

When they finished, Jen reread their notes out loud. She sighed with disgust and threw the papers on the desk. "That was about zero help."

"We must be missing something," Zeke said thoughtfully. "Did we forget to write down a clue?"

Jen shook her head. "I don't think so. We'll just have to figure it out tomorrow. . . . I just hope we're not too late."

Note to Reader

Have you figured out who else is on the hunt for the treasure? Jen and Zeke have made pretty good notes on the suspects, but they did miss a few very important clues. Without those clues, it's almost impossible to figure out who the mysterious treasure hunter is.

Have you come to a conclusion? Take your time. Carefully review the suspect sheets. Fill in any details Jen and Zeke missed. When you think you have a solution, read the last chapter to find out if Jen and Zeke can put all the pieces together to solve *The Mystery of the Dark Lighthouse*.

Good luck!

Solution

Another Mystery Solved!

Zeke slept fitfully that night. He dreamed about large, ornate keys and old-fashioned sailing ships. When it was finally time to get up, he was thrilled to see that the rest of the clouds had disappeared and the sun was shining brightly. The storm was over!

He flicked his light switch, but the power was still off. He knew it'd be back on shortly. He threw on his clothes and banged on Jen's door on his way down the stairs. She came out of her room looking bleary-eyed. Slinky darted down the stairs.

"I had the worst dreams last night," she admitted when Zeke said she looked tired. "Catherine kept leading me into the tunnels and then leaving me all alone in the dark. It was so spooky."

"It was probably just her ghost telling you to hurry up and find the treasure," Zeke teased.

Before Jen could respond, they were in the dining room and Karen was hurrying over to them. "Guess what," she whispered. "The key is gone!"

"What?" Jen exclaimed.

"Shhhh."

"Someone stole the key out of your room last night?" Zeke asked.

"No, no," Karen said soothingly. "I still have the treasure chest key. I mean the one in the hall closet that I was locked in. Remember how you said it looked like the one we found?" she reminded Jen.

The twins nodded.

"Well, on my way down here this morning, I wanted to compare them, but the key is missing from the closet door. I'll bet the thief stole the key to try it in the treasure chest!"

"That means we don't have much time," Zeke said urgently. "Sometimes those old locks will open even if the key isn't the exact one made for the lock. We have to find that treasure before whoever it is tries the key."

"That means we have to go into the tunnels now," Jen said, glancing around to make sure no one was eavesdropping.

"Let's go," Karen said. "I took my mom's flashlight and I have the key. We have to hurry."

Slipping quietly and, they hoped, unnoticed into the kitchen, the three of them hurried to the secret door in the pantry. Jen took a deep breath before following the other two into the murky darkness. Even with the flashlight, it seemed spooky in the tunnels.

At the bottom of the stairs, Zeke stopped them. "I thought I heard something."

They all froze and listened.

"I don't hear anything," Jen finally whispered.

Zeke shrugged doubtfully. "Okay, let's go, but be as quiet as you can."

At the second fork in the path, they decided to check the storage room. The room was empty. Then they retraced their steps and stood at the fork again.

"Look!" Zeke crouched down and examined the floor. "See these drag marks?"

Jen leaned over and peered at the ground. "It looks like someone was dragging a heavy chest."

"I bet that's what we heard yesterday," Karen said. "The marks lead down there." She pointed.

No one said anything for a second. The drag marks led straight to the set of stairs that led even deeper underground.

"Where does this path lead?" Jen whispered.

"I don't know," Karen admitted. "Remember, I was too chicken to check it out."

Zeke stood up. "We're about to find out. Come on."

Jen felt as if she were being buried alive as she stepped down and down and down. The stairs were never-ending. The air got colder and there was definitely a strong breeze. They thought that they must have been getting closer to the ocean, because the sound of crashing waves was getting louder and louder.

After what seemed like an hour, they reached the bottom of the stairs.

"I think I know where we are." Zeke had to raise his voice to be heard over the sound of the waves. "These are the caves at the bottom of the cliffs. When the tide is in, like now, the caves are hidden, but at low tide you can get into them from the shore."

"This must have been how Catherine's father hid all the treasure from the wrecked ships," Jen said. "He dragged it from the sea into these caves and then carried it up through the secret tunnels."

Karen flashed the light back and forth. "Let's look around."

Zeke stopped and cocked his head.

"What is it?" Jen asked.

"I keep thinking I hear something."

"The ocean," Jen said.

Zeke shrugged. "Must be."

The underground caves were divided into three

parts. One part was a huge cavern where the kids couldn't see the ceiling. Sprouting off that cave there was a low tunnel that led to a smaller cave filled with glittering crystals.

"Are these diamonds?" Jen breathed in awe.

"No," Zeke said. "Probably just salt crystals."

Another low tunnel led down to the opening of the cave. But because the tide was high, the passage soon became flooded.

"We'd better not go this way," Zeke said. "We'll have to come back when the tide is out and the ocean is calm. It's still churned up from the storm."

Jen quickly agreed, not eager to get her feet sopping wet. They all turned around and inspected the third section of the cave, which was on the far wall of the huge cavern. It was honeycombed with small, shallow caves that had been dug out of the wall. Each cave was big enough to fit two or three seated people. Jen counted at least ten of these strange indentations in the wall.

"Look!" Karen shouted. She shone her light on the far left hole.

Jen's heart pounded louder than the waves with excitement as the three of them rushed over to a treasure chest partly hidden in one of the small caverns. Someone had tried to tuck the chest as far back as possible, but it was too big and bulky to hide completely.

They crouched down in front of it. With shaking fingers, Karen withdrew the old key from her pocket.

"Stop right there!" someone shouted behind them.

The three of them whirled around.

"You!" Zeke exclaimed.

Professor Snyder shrugged. "I knew you kids would find the treasure sooner or later. I'm glad that you did. Now give me the key." He held out his hand.

A flicker of light behind the professor caught Jen's eye. She grabbed the key from Karen as the Professor stepped forward.

"No," Jen cried. "You can't have it."

The professor took a menacing step toward her. "Give it to me now. I don't have time for this."

There was a sudden clatter from the tunnel. Professor Snyder whipped around to see what the noise was.

Mrs. Mills stepped forward. "The key belongs to my daughter and her friends," Mrs. Mills said sharply. "I suggest you stay right there," she threatened when the professor looked as if he might lunge at her. "The police are right behind me." She dug a length of rope from her back pocket and tossed it to Zeke. "Tie him up."

Zeke grinned. This weekend wasn't turning out so badly after all! As he moved forward with the rope in his hands, Aunt Bee and Detective Wilson stumbled into the stone cavern.

"What's going on?" Aunt Bee exclaimed.

Detective Wilson immediately hurried over to help Zeke. It took only five minutes to explain what had happened.

Grinning, Jen finally said, "Let's get this treasure up to the B&B. I'm dying to see what's inside."

It took quite a bit of lugging and hauling to heave the chest up all the stairs and through the tunnels into the pantry. They finally pulled it into the dining room. The other guests heard the commotion and gathered around.

"The treasure!" Esther exclaimed. "How absolutely, positively perfect!"

"Is that really it?" Jaspar asked, taking a closer look at the old chest.

"We think so," Zeke said.

Mrs. Snyder came into the room at that moment and cried out in dismay. "I knew this wouldn't work. I told you not to sneak around like that," she said to her husband.

Professor Snyder bowed his head sheepishly. "I only wanted it for research, but the more I hunted for it, the more gold and jewels I imagined in the chest. I knew that Jacob Markham had wrecked ships and plundered them. I started to get as greedy as he was. I'm sorry. I'm sorry I sneaked around and stole the photograph. I guess I was possessed by treasure fever. I even searched your room," he added, glancing at Karen and her mother.

Mrs. Snyder shook her head. "I guess I might as well admit to everyone that I'm not really hard of hearing. I'm sorry I lied to you all."

"I knew it," Zeke said. "You were the lookout for the professor."

Mrs. Snyder nodded. "That's right. Whenever he got too loud digging in the tunnels, I started coughing and sneezing to warn him. I pretended to be hard of hearing because I knew if you heard the noises and noticed I started coughing every time, eventually you would put two and two together."

Jen remembered the time she'd heard a strange noise that stopped after Mrs. Snyder's sneezing attack. It all made sense now. She turned to the professor again. "And you kept some clothes and boots in the tunnels to wear while you were digging around, right?"

The professor nodded. "I didn't want my dirty, dusty clothes or shoes to give me away."

"But your socks did," Zeke interjected. "We saw them in your room when we were cleaning. I just didn't figure out why your socks were so dirty until it was too late," he admitted.

"What about you?" Jen asked, turning to Mrs. Mills. "How did you find us in time?"

"Oh, I knew you kids were up to something. Aunt Bee keeps this place really clean, so I couldn't figure out why the three of you had dirty shoes all the time. I finally figured out there really must be tunnels in this place. So I did a little sleuthing of my own and found the secret entrance to the tunnels. In fact, remember that moaning sound you heard?"

The three kids nodded.

"That was because of me. I left the pantry door open a little so I could find my way out. I never dreamed it would create a wind tunnel and cause all that noise. When I heard you coming, I ran away. I didn't want you to think I didn't trust you and was spying on you," she said, looking at Karen.

"But you found the tunnels before we did," Jen said. "Because I picked up your missing button in there the first time Zeke and I were in there."

Mrs. Mills frowned. "I was missing that button long before I found the secret entrance. How strange."

Slinky meowed loudly and rubbed against Jen's leg. Jen laughed and picked up the cat. "You little thief. Slinky must have been playing with the button when she got stuck in the tunnels."

"This morning," Mrs. Mills continued her story, "I saw you three disappear, then I noticed the professor following you. I didn't know exactly what was going on, but I thought I should keep an eye on things. I followed Professor Snyder as he followed you."

"And it's a good thing you brought rope," Jen said, laughing.

Mrs. Mills grinned. "I had it with me to tie down the loose luggage rack on the rental car. It knocked all the way here from the airport and nearly drove me crazy. I was going to tie it down before we headed back to the airport this afternoon."

Aunt Bee shuddered. "I'm so glad I had no idea all of this was going on. I'm old enough as it is."

Zeke hugged his aunt. "You saved the day," he told her. "If you and Detective Wilson hadn't come to the rescue, who knows what might have happened."

"How did you know about the tunnels anyway?" Jen asked.

Aunt Bee looked at her. "I just happened to see Mrs. Mills wander into the kitchen. I followed her, thinking she was looking for something else to eat. When she disappeared into the pantry, I rushed to get Detective Wilson. Luckily he was here early today to help with the roof leak on the third floor. Anyway, we found the secret door in the pantry and followed the sound of talking until we reached you." She put a hand over her heart. "I'm just so glad we arrived in time."

"Me, too," Jen said. Then she flung a hand toward the chest. "Let's open the treasure!" She couldn't stand another second of suspense.

Karen took out the key and inserted it into the lock. Jen and Zeke held their breath as Karen turned the key. Click.

Moving slowly, as though afraid that a ghost would jump out at her, Karen lifted the lid.

Everyone gasped. No wonder the trunk had been so heavy and hard to lug up the stairs. It was full to the brim with golden cups and pieces of jewelry. There were necklaces with pearls the size of marbles, and even a dagger with diamonds and rubies embedded in the hilt.

Karen ignored all the jewels and reached for a pile of leather-bound books. "The rest of Catherine's diaries," she breathed with satisfaction. She started thumbing through them as the rest of the group sifted through the unbelievable treasure.

"There must be over a million dollars' worth of stuff in here," Zeke said.

Deeper in the trunk there wasn't as much gold and jewelry, but there were lengths of fabric with gold thread sewn through them and old-fashioned shoes with pearl buttons that looked like new. There were three silver mirrors that were tarnished nearly black, but Jen could tell from the intricately carved frames and handles that they would be beautiful when polished.

"This is almost as exciting as uncovering the Egyptian tomb," Jaspar commented.

Zeke asked him, "You never had anything to do with hunting for the treasure, did you?"

The TV reporter cleared his throat. "Well, I do admit I was intrigued. I followed you kids to the library without your knowing it."

Jen and Zeke looked at each other and grinned, but didn't interrupt.

"Then I took out the book you'd looked at," Jaspar continued. "But it didn't have much information in it. I was going to search a little more for the treasure, thinking it'd be fun, but then my producer called about my next story and I've been busy working on it ever since."

"Your story had nothing to do with the treasure?" Jen asked.

"Of course not," Jaspar said, looking a bit insulted. "I have to go for *big* stories."

Karen laughed. "We think this *is* a big story."

"I'm afraid it wouldn't bring in the ratings," Jaspar said.

"Why were you trying to talk to Esther all the time?" Jen asked, a little upset that he thought

Mystic, Maine, wasn't big enough to do a story about.

Jaspar glanced at Esther and shrugged. "I'm afraid that's not for me to say. I promised."

Esther sighed and rolled her eyes. "Oh, I may as well tell you, since you feel like family now." In one graceful sweep, she pulled off her straight black hair. Under the wig she had short blond hair.

"Esther Barrimore!" Aunt Bee cried. "The famous mystery author. I love your books. I knew you looked familiar!"

Esther smiled. "Yes, I'm afraid I've been living a bit of a lie. I came here as Esther Barr to get away for a few days. But as soon as I got here I realized this is the perfect setting for my next mystery. I've been taking notes like crazy. I didn't want Jaspar, who has interviewed me a number of times and recognized me right away, to blow my cover. When people find out who I am they want to ask me all sorts of questions, and I never get any work done."

"Do you happen to take notes on a miniature tape recorder?" Zeke asked.

"How did you know that? I thought I had hidden it from everyone."

Zeke grinned. "I saw it running in your room when we were cleaning and you were asking all those questions. And you must have been recording ideas for the mystery when I overheard you talking about the treasure yesterday after breakfast."

Esther patted him on the back. "You are quite the detective, young man. Perhaps I'll have to put you in my next book."

Jen took a turn to add her own clues. "When you said you'd just washed your hair, you really hadn't, had you?"

"No," Esther admitted. "I just put the towel on to cover my real hair when you knocked on my door. The wig wasn't as easy to put on as a towel was. And I have another awful confession to make."

Everyone waited expectantly while Esther took a deep breath. She turned to Karen. "I was the one who locked you in the closet. I was out of my room and I heard you coming. I couldn't let you see me without my wig on, so I pushed you in the closet. You didn't get hurt, did you?"

Karen shook her head.

"I went to put on my wig and then I was going to let you out, but you were already gone when I came back. I am so sorry."

Karen smiled. "It's okay. I was only in there a couple of minutes."

Esther sighed with relief. "And you probably thought I was a real snoop, but I was just trying to get a feeling for the B&B and how it runs and looks."

Jen grinned. "We were wondering when we caught you looking for a pen and they were right there in front of you."

Esther blushed. "It's the curse of a writer to be nosy!"

Professor Snyder coughed. "What's going to happen to me?"

Detective Wilson frowned. "You didn't hurt anyone and you don't have a weapon. But you did steal the photograph and the clue." He turned to Aunt Bee. "Do you want to press any charges?"

Aunt Bee sighed. "No. Treasure and riches certainly do bring out the worst in people. Let him go."

Detective Wilson untied the professor and, with heads bowed in shame, the Snyders left to pack their bags.

"Listen to this," Karen said. She removed a loose sheet of paper from one of the diaries. "Catherine wrote this when she was seventy-six. '*Herein lie my diaries. I have lived a full life with thirteen children, twenty-seven grandchildren, and four great-grandchildren. Over the years, I have used Father's ill-begotten riches to help the poor and needy. I pray that whoever finds this will continue to offer help where it is needed. When you think of my father, Jacob Markham, think not with malice and scorn, but know that he did repent and never again did the lighthouse go dark.'* She signed it and dated it 1966."

No one spoke. Jen tried to imagine the young girl in front of the Christmas tree growing old, giving away money, probably in secret, to those who needed it. She blinked back the tears that filled her eyes. Even though she knew it was impossible, she wished there were some way she could have known Catherine Markham.

"I think the treasure should stay here," Karen said thoughtfully. She turned to Aunt Bee. "Will you make sure the right people get it?"

"Certainly," Aunt Bee said. Zeke could see that his aunt was touched. "Are you sure?"

Karen nodded. "The money should stay in Mystic and be given back to the descendants of the lost sailors."

Aunt Bee nodded. "I agree, and I'm sure I'll find a fair way to distribute the funds, perhaps college scholarships, and new books for the library, and . . ."

Jen laughed, jerking her thumb in her aunt's direction. "She won't have any problem sharing the wealth, that's for sure."

Karen smiled and gently rubbed her hand over the worn leather bindings. "I just want these diaries."

Suddenly, all the lights in the B&B blazed on. The group cheered.

"Treasure and electricity in one day!" Zeke said, laughing.

"Can't get richer than that," Jen added with a smile.

✓

Later that afternoon, Jen and Zeke waved good-bye as all the guests left. As the last car drove off down the long driveway, Jen sighed. "This wasn't such a bad weekend after all."

On the way to her room, Jen stopped to look at the photo of Catherine Markham standing in front of the Christmas tree. She rubbed her eyes, sure she was imagining it. But it seemed to her that Catherine's smile was a lot wider than it had been before.

About the Author

Laura E. Williams has written more than twenty-five books for children, her most recent being YOU SOLVE IT: *The Mystery of Dead Man's Curve*, *ABC Kids*, and *The Executioner's Daughter*. In her spare time she works on her rubber art stamp company she started in her garage.

Ms. Williams loves lighthouses. Someday she hopes to visit a lighthouse bed-and-breakfast just like the one in Mystic, Maine.

Mystic Lighthouse

Suspect Sheet

Name:

Motive:

Clues: